T0277832

The World Machine

THE ITALIAN LIST

Paolo Volponi

The World Machine

TRANSLATED BY
RICHARD DIXON

LONDON NEW YORK CALCUTTA

The Italian List

SERIES EDITOR: ALBERTO TOSCANO

This book has been translated thanks to a translation grant awarded by the
Italian Ministry of Foreign Affairs and International Cooperation.

Questo libro è stato tradotto grazie a un contributo alla traduzione assegnato
dal Ministero degli Affari Esteri e della Cooperazione Internazionale italiano.

Seagull Books, 2024

First published in Italian as *La macchina mondiale* by Paolo Volponi

© 1975, 2013 and 2015 Giulio Einaudi editore s.p.a., Torino

English translation and Afterword © Richard Dixon, 2024

ISBN   978 1 8030 9 376 5

British Library Cataloguing-in-Publication Data

A catalogue record for this book is available from the British Library

Typeset at Seagull Books, Calcutta, India

Printed and bound in the USA by Integrated Books International

CONTENTS

All the people and events in this story are inventions; none of the various cultural and historical references are intended to relate to actual occurrences.

The main character's thoughts about creation and rebirth are derived from those being developed and organized, along with other ideas, by signor P.M.V. in his treatise on the Constitution of a New Academy of Friendship among Qualified People.

The passages in italics in this novel have been taken freely from this treatise, though with much respect to its original spirit.

Those wishing to gain a fuller understanding of the theories set out in the treatise may, through the author, contact Signor P.M.V. who will be most willing to provide all information and clarification, having waited many years for an opportunity to consult with students and colleagues and to seek their advice, to collaborate with scientists, and to interest publishers.

My thought and my material being, the internal ructions they produce in the design of my machine and the operation of its various switches, still bind me to those things and events that go on around me, in my house and on my land, and in this piece of Marche countryside near the Apennines that is called the parish of San Savino. Things around here move very slowly, or swiftly vanish, unnoticed and as if by chance; and there is no order to them, just as these hills and these crags have no order, these ditches and gullies that go from San Savino towards Frontone or Monlione or Acquaviva. Yet the rows of vines, the lanes, the chimney smoke and reflections of the windowpanes often together form a grid, especially on a Sunday, which might seem the outline for a mechanical design, in other words, an attempt at perfection and happiness.

Around here, different concretions of matter, different strata are still found merged, and I am constantly finding a pebble, a small flint blade, or a fossil, which has led me to feel that I'm on a strip of land whose people have never seen much progress and have never performed great deeds, a strip of land still cut off and still bearing the marks of natural phenomena that scour them: rain and wind, snow and storms.

To me, this strip of land seems close to the origin, close to the great mouth, and maybe for this, observing its elementary composition, I have come to understand those things that I understand and am writing down in another book besides this one, in a treatise on philosophy and mechanics which can explain the destiny of mankind as well as the reasons for its position in the universe, and may identify the procedures for its liberation and for the *constitution of a new academy of friendship* among all people of the earth once they have recognized and declared *the validity of the psychological arguments, the rules for the instruments of science, and have forged an automatism that respects and exploits the integrity and energy of every force.*

This book, however, which I offer to readers as something they can read after a day's work, or while relaxing, or during a momentary pause, will explain my own particular fate, as well as my beliefs and my propositions which have never been ill-conceived: for example, the questions that have arisen around me and the trial at which I was convicted and for which I am waiting for the appeal that should be heard in the next few months at the Court in Urbino.

Even with these few words of explanation I haven't yet said what I will say right now, and as directly and forcefully as if I were unscrewing a valve and letting hot water out of a radiator. By which I mean my father running off, which has reduced me to living alone in this village of San Savino, and a life in this house abandoned even by my wife who has also gone off to live it up in Rome after telling everyone about my ill-treatment, with so much cruel invention of a truth that has led to me being publicly denounced and then dragged into court.

But to tell the whole story in proper order, so as not to get carried away by my own hot air and then lose track and forget what I'm saying, I must start with those early days during which my ideas began to emerge. From those harsh and sublime days during which the mechanisms of my brain found in the peace and quiet, in the right humidity, in the friendly and inspiring buzz of insects around the grape, in the shade where I was resting at that summer's end, now that much work had been done and now that even my father had given up hope that I might go back to retake the exam for my lower-school certificate . . . the mechanisms of my young brain found the first trace of my discovery: when my inner circulation seemed almost to abandon my body and find another route, to invent other circuits around the margin of my head, practically between my head and the root of the oaks and the elms at the edge of the vineyard, beyond the support posts in the vineyard that I myself had put in: on that hummock where I lay after my meal at home and where I felt better in myself, precisely because I had discovered it was touched by a breeze, as if there were an air vent that came up from a great pipe. I gazed at my feet and realized that somebody had constructed them.

In such moments, it was so important to recognize that concept of construction and to begin to look at the sky over the branches of the elms and the vines, like looking at a road, like the route taken by a creator, which must then be the route taken by many, with crowds of footprints, not of one single creator but of a multitude of creators—in other words, of a primary, absent population that was watching from a distance, all with celestial blue eyes, or who weren't watching at all, hardly noticing us, the smaller and less sentient population, with their antennae and almost deactivated, making a cursory check, as happens in February to the farmer who certainly won't bother going to see whether the ears of corn have yet formed or whether they're in danger of being pecked by shrikes.

In my treatise I have written: *Automaton, Creator = Homo sapiens*; *Automaton, not creator = mineral and vegetable kingdom*; and there's a series of diagrams showing the anatomy of the vast machinery of creation and the infinite method of creation.

And at the end of the first page, I have written: *Just as the yield in any automatic device fluctuates between a maximum and a minimum, so too in every object there is a fluctuation between two extremes which simultaneously produces the result and, by interacting with each other, moves it forward.*

During that period, I fluctuated much. I shook and felt as flimsy and restless as the wing or indeed the whole body of a wasp, and the more I fluctuated the more I felt the construction of the machine clearly within me, felt the principles of mechanics—above all, the construction of my own machine, in the movement of a leg, of a knee, in an elbow and a knee joint and in a sudden spasm, which always started from the slightest impulse that I could trigger from an inner switch above my eyes: inner, inside, imperceptible, nonetheless triggered, and which I could feel triggering in that silence like the movement of an eyebrow, like another of the movements of the tiny body of that wasp on the grape.

That period marked the beginning of my own story, in the form of various endeavours to assemble and substantiate my thoughts, in other words, my ideas, by questioning the local priest and other people, looking for books to read on science and particularly mathematics, trying to approach my father and mother, and also the Contessa Carsidoni, who lived in her villa on the other side of the hill at Canneto, who had been a friend of Marconi and had many books, many maps and charts of the whole world in her house in the city and her villa at Canneto too.

Contessa Carsidoni was the first person to warn my father about my studies after she had banished me from her library, telling me that the most important answers are to be found in the Catechism and, once those answers had been understood and memorized, the most important thing is purity of heart, which also means pious and healthy labour and respect for the world.

My father was waiting for me with a strap and taught me a lesson in beating; and from underneath I could see how each blow crossed the brim of his hat and his eyes, and how his expression darkened more and more, and how he must have felt inside, even if all flow and external contact had stopped, yet he must have felt it . . . his breath heaved in so many spasmodic *uh*'s that came down with the sound of each last lash, a sound like that made by a pond after some object had dropped in and after the water had settled, and the mud beneath it too: and that sound made by the pond means there's a break in this space that the fallen object had as its own and which it was outwardly destined to have between earth and air . . . my father must have understood too, for something must certainly have snapped inside him each time he moved his arm or repeated his resolve to hurt, and he must have understood he was contravening the forces of life and seeking to break something he hadn't built and did not own, and which was alive and had its own space and its own separate rules outside those rules that were his, which bore no relation to his rules, since he chose to deny them with such violence, which he repeatedly did.

What I can say is that the creators have built one machine the same as another, giving them all the same rules and even the awareness of these rules, while not wishing to give all machines a shared rule that resides in the very consciousness of the community, of possible communion and then of converting all rules towards a purpose that might also be achieved, and would then be most attractive— that of a rebellion against creators, of a liberation from mechanics with the invention of a supermechanics and therefore of a superbody. Unless, of course, creators are so disinterested as to have no interest in the fate of these machines, invented by them for a purpose which then came to an end or was itself idle and futile from the beginning; or that the creators themselves then died out, maybe transferring something of themselves into their machines.

But I reject idleness and futility, I who have often been regarded as idle and futile because for some time I have followed only my thoughts and the interpretation of the principles that I was exploring word by word, sign by sign on this earth, in people themselves, in my neighbours and in their lives; I who, for my part, consider the work that my father did so shoddily to be idle and futile, in other words, harmful and pointless, and also all the work of the servants around the Contessa. But the days passed, giving me some proof each day, and some result, and tying me more and more to my own discovery which was, day by day, more and more exact, and which bound me more and more to all things, to everything in and around San Savino, on the hillocks or at the foot of a hollow, whether it were far away, up in the sky, over the mountains, in the splendour of the constellations, or once the summer was over, with the passing of some migratory bird or flocks of skylarks and thrushes.

But if I return to those days I must return to what happened, even at the risk of putting aside the treatise and ending only the day before the end of my life, and I need to start explaining, for this too is relevant, all the more if it is my intention and my hope, with regard to others who must be moved to listen, to prepare a footstool so that people can climb more easily onto the mechanism of my treatise; to explain also because in many details there is scientific proof of my treatise, of the dynamics and of the consequentiality of every arrangement of words and numbers with the inventions I was discovering like every good inventor, all happening around me and which I was merely connecting with my own life, and with all physical life.

In the early days, the first evidence came from Mordi's bankruptcy in Cagli, and then the disappearance of his manager, who was my father. He ran off from San Savino to Rome with my mother—to Rome, somewhere near Maccarese, to run one of the estates belonging to Prince Torlonia. Then my meeting with Massimina at Pergola; then my visits and frequent presence at Serra

Sant'Abbondio where Massimina lived; the political discussions there; my argument with the parish priest and the monk at the church; my final expulsion from the village by a group of people who attacked me with stones. Massimina married me all the same, maybe after the monk and that same group of stone throwers had connived and plotted to ensure our marriage would mark the beginning of my downfall, even if Massimina loved me and I loved her, as I still do, even after she had run away, also to Rome, into the service of the Consigliere.

WITNESS DEPOSITION

SUMMARY PROCEEDINGS

On the fourteenth day of September 1959 at Pergola, appearing before Dottor Luciano Garbarini, Deputy Magistrate—the witness Sergio Diotallevi, labourer, born at Canneto near Pergola on 5-5-1925 and resident there, who to each question duly responded:

—Regarding the relations between Anteo Crocioni and his wife Massimina Meleschi, I can state only that not many months after their wedding, Crocioni slapped his wife in the presence of workers who were in a field belonging to the said Crocioni.

—I was working in my field some hundred metres below when I saw Anteo Crocioni push his wife at a point where there was greater risk of slipping and falling, causing her to drop the basket she was carrying on her head which contained food for the workers in the fields.

—There is nothing else I can say directly about relations between the couple in question since I am often away from the village for my work.

—I have nothing else to add.

L.C.S. Signed

Sergio Diotallevi

Chiesa, Court Clerk

Deputy Magistrate

(Signature not legible)

WITNESS DEPOSITION

SUMMARY PROCEEDINGS

On the fourteenth day of September 1959 at Pergola, appearing before Dottor Luciano Garbarini, Deputy Magistrate—Vilfredo De Angelis, aka Lindone, born at Buonconsiglio, Frontone, on 6/2/1924, resident at San Savino, machine operator, who to each question duly responded:

—I live close to where Anteo Crocioni and his wife Massimina Meleschi lived. As to their relations, I can state that for at least the period of their cohabitation Anteo Crocioni was well known throughout the village for being a violent and obstinate man, quarrelsome as well as lazy, particularly towards his wife Massimina Meleschi; lazy to the point of spending whole days lying on the ground face up or walking round and round all day in a patch of sand holding a cane as if he were looking for some precious stone, or not leaving the house for weeks, not even after a storm had damaged his crops.

—I have no direct knowledge of the arguments and ill-treatment that Crocioni is said to have inflicted on his wife. All I can say is that Massimina Meleschi asked me one day to take her to her family home at Serra Sant'Abbondio and told me on that occasion that her husband Anteo Crocioni had struck her repeatedly for trivial reasons, pointing as proof of her allegations to a bruise above her knee. Yes, on the thigh.

—I can say no more since, being a machine operator, I am often away from home for my work and when I get back late at night in the summer or in the morning without sleep, I certainly haven't time to think about Crocioni's wickedness. One day, before the sun was up, I found him in a daze by his front door, drawing on the wall, and I remember him saying to me, 'Machine operator, I'm designing a machine that you have never tried, nor will you ever try.'

—I have nothing else to add.

WITNESS DEPOSITION

SUMMARY PROCEEDINGS

On the fourteenth day of September 1959 at Pergola, appearing before Dottor Luciano Garbarini assisted by the undersigned Court Clerk, Eusebio Astorri, born at San Savino, Frontone, on 24/7/1929 and resident there—dealer [trading in nothing, a job invented by the Christian Democrats!] who to each question duly responded:

—Regarding the relationship existing between Anteo Crocioni and his wife Massimina Meleschi on which His Honour is questioning me, I can say that such relations have always been exceedingly tense, due above all to the violent and hot-headed character of Crocioni who, for some time after their wedding, ill-treated his wife with beatings of various kinds and abusive words. Given the proximity of my house to that of Crocioni, Massimina Meleschi often appeared in public with bruises to her face from her husband's beatings. I can further state that Crocioni's violent scenes generally took place inside his house.

—So far as violence that I could witness, I can state that several months after their marriage, while I was working in my field close by, Anteo Crocioni attacked his wife by slapping and beating her while she was labouring hard on the piece of land belonging to her husband about forty metres from where I was watching. I cannot say what reasons Anteo Crocioni had for adopting such behaviour.

—All acts of violence of the kind described took place during their period of cohabitation between 1956 and 1957.

—I have no more to add.

The witness Rosanna Meleschi is called. When questioned she duly responded:

—I am Rosanna Meleschi—born 22–7–1946 at Serra Sant' Abbondio and residing there, sister of the complainant.

On being questioned about Para. 6:

—I remember that one day in autumn 1956 I was at the house of Anteo Crocioni when he repeatedly punched and slapped my sister. I do not know what reason he had to hit her and why he was so angry. I was only eleven at the time, and so frightened that I started crying. I don't think anyone else was present. (The witness is paid 440 lire.)

I must say immediately, it seems strange to me that people who come out with such lies can exist in a small village such as mine, can live there so far away from everywhere and with the land I have described; people who behave like enemies to their own siblings, to those who work their own land; people who can behave as if they were ignorant of any kind of destiny and who have never understood the significance of any way forward, as if they had never seen a star cross the sky and a path open up through the sky or in the snow, when all seems locked and bolted, or the path of any kind of insect or drop of water or pebble, and how in the end this pebble depends on friendship with those things it finds so it can rest in its place. These friends, these people I see walking, people I know and love like a part of my day and of the whole machinery, have clearly never thought about an academy of happiness, have never attempted to understand human destiny, and have never looked at the countryside, nor even at humanity. Perhaps they have looked at men and women only as enemies or as family relations or as lovers, in other words, blinded by a predominant feeling, and never as a possible subject for meditation and awareness, or as a creator that might do something different, that might move, exist, behave differently from what they themselves in that moment have in mind and believe and regard as significant for the conduct of that being whom they are watching. And they certainly haven't ever looked even at their town and countryside to see whether beyond this town there is further countryside and beyond the countryside there are streets and piazzas, and houses too, and whether the houses in the town are detached or built against the town walls or propped against each other or separated by streets that are wide and level or steep, whether in the middle of the same old small piazza there are shops, and whether at one corner of that piazza there is a church, or whether there are large blocks of houses and courtyards made of brick and stone and whether all of these are inhabited; and how it is all in the open air and enjoys the sun from dawn to dusk and how it is ventilated by healthy breezes and positioned on high ground so as to catch the pleasant aroma of the valleys, and of ripening fruits, and so as to have vegetable gardens sloping in such a way that each plant doesn't block the other and doesn't deprive it of sun and rain and wind.

They have never looked at how this poor humanity is governed in effect only by itself, how those in power are far away and how the smell of their posters is damper and darker, lashed by hostile winds and pinned to the walls with strange official seals that still look like the traces of a fascist machine gun. How government means easy and possible everyday access and the opening and closing of that door and that window and meeting together, and looking at trees, and thus encouraging the construction and the use of the machine and giving the machine its proper position in the evolution of the species.

They have never considered how in order to survive it is enough just to eat and to reproduce, but how in order to *exist* one has to reconstruct oneself each day, one has to obey a superior law that governs the universe embodied and living in the bodies of organic matter, and requiring that these bodies construct others in order to develop themselves conceptually, to explore the great explosion which is the universe, its rotating flight which is the great pattern of life. Otherwise, if we were inert like those who have spoken in this way before the justices and who live inertly in my village, we would be no more than a mistake, a badly built machine.

At the age of fifteen I had the good fortune to start thinking, at twenty to start writing. At night, during the summer, when I was fifteen, I felt a discontentment as I slept, as I tried to sleep; or I slept while keeping a consciousness outside myself, just as a machine can be switched off but with a small light still on. I felt a discontentment in my thoughts, felt uneasy as my fingers scratched the mattress and the bedsprings, and I felt that great void beneath the bed like an immense abyss, like that pointless emptiness a man feels if he cannot give some meaning to his separation from his mother, knocked to the ground and crying and trying to get back up. I felt this great pointless emptiness, this unease, as if fleas and other insects were also crawling about, as if ideas of the divinity and unity of creation were pointless.

I felt so discontented but gradually so strong and powerful as to think that I might rid myself of those fleas and of that emptiness and begin, myself, to emit, and then to harness, an energy that was not only fluid and spontaneous but also as controlled and orderly as a programme, as a coherent chain that I could cast out or pull back in.

From there, from that night for many nights, I continued to order my thoughts and to plan around myself. Indeed, as I wrote in my treatise, *Those who have designed man as a machine couldn't give him a programme with one instinct as they did to animals, because while animals had to remain always the same, man had to repeat the work of his designers, but with different materials and forms, he would therefore have to get there through a long apprenticeship, satisfying the passions and ambitions determined by his life in the world, which draw man towards a goal that is unknown to him but well known to those who have willed it.*

If only my fellow inhabitants, who are always shaking their heads, who are never happy, always struggling and taking one step forward and one back, if only they had considered their same conclusion that 'the world is a whore'; if only they had realized as they walked up and down and had understood on meeting each other, studying for a moment their hands, their feet, and the land, the poor innocent land, that 'someone is taking advantage', then they could have gone on and might have reached the conclusion that there are other worlds and other lands, these likewise happy or unhappy, which become extinct or flourish, or where forms of life die out so that those who have produced and controlled them emigrate with their being, with their essence carried into other guises that may also be human. This might explain how fathers and sons then follow the same paths and often fall at the same point, and how even the lessons of history have never served any purpose, at least not until now, and how these same lessons have been distorted and obstructed by classes of selfish people, by those who are inferior, imperfect machines, and who are afraid of being so and having to choose the road ahead.

One day that summer, as I was wrestling with my thoughts inside that void and began to see beside me the light of the strength of those thoughts as well as that void, not yet knowing how to guide the light and how to let it shine, I met a young man quietly bathing at the river near Canneto, hidden among the bracken. He was pale and kept his hands in the water and had a look of enchantment on his face, as though searching under the water for a pebble or something that interested him. Maybe he was searching out his fear, since his throat was tight, around his ears and his shoulders, and his chest was as hollow as a basin and he moved slowly, rigidly, after long pauses, because of the same fear that gripped him. Or maybe it was the coldness of the water. Or his fear might have been simply the fear of drowning and not of me or of something supernatural.

I had taken the mule to drink at that point of the river. The women were further back with their baskets of laundry. I led the mule into the water and began to wash it. I did so to muddy the water and to see if that pale youth would get out and reveal what his fear was. I saw him moving about in the water, wading towards the bank across the deepest pool where the current of water I was muddying didn't reach him. I saw him get out of the river, holding one arm in front and one behind and his body hunched, and realized then that his fear might have been about his nakedness, and more than anything about his paleness, which moved over him like an animal. A moment later he was dressing behind the bush and slipped on a pair of tight breeches and a pair of long black cotton socks that reached up to the buttons of his trousers. He was a seminarian, in black and white, standing behind the bush with his sunken chest. I called across.

'Hello, you look like a student.'

'No, I'm at the seminary,' he replied.

'All right, you're a student at the seminary.'

'I am.'

'So, tell me,' I shouted from the middle of the current, 'if someone thinks that men are not creatures of heaven, but machines built by other men, or even by other beings who live somewhere else or are even extinct, is it better for him to study mechanical sciences or philosophy to prove this theory of his?'

The seminarian turned and looked at me. 'But someone who's interested in such ideas, hasn't he already studied?' he asked.

'No, he has studied nothing,' I said.

'Then study will be pointless, I'm afraid.'

'Why,' I asked, 'are you another servant of the nobility?'

'No,' he answered, 'but if your question is sincere, I think such an inventor is a philosopher more than anything, and it would make no difference whether he has studied or not, though he could still study philosophy, theoretical philosophy.'

'Ah, but wait a moment,' I said, 'wait there, behind that bush. I want you to tell me about theoretical philosophy and what to read. Maybe you have some of those books, maybe you have them with your clothes, behind the bush.'

I led the mule back to the Canneto bank and crossed the river to the other side, to the Montevecchio bank. When I reached the seminarian, he had already put on a collarless striped cotton shirt. His chest was now heaving for breath and his pale, blue wrists were crossed over his knees. I sat down before him to put him at ease.

'Do you know the name of this river?' I asked.

He looked back at the hill as if to check that the woods and the hill were still in their place above us, with those immense green and blue shadows where, in the chestnut and oak woods, there seemed to be nobody and no road. Indeed, I had never heard any-one talk of people at Montevecchio and had never even imagined, looking at that mountain from a distance, covered by the thick silk of those shadows, that there might be a village with houses. The seminarian looked back at me.

'The river here is the Cinisco,' he said, 'a small river that rises at Petrara, above Frontone.'

'You know a lot of things,' I said. 'Let me see the book on theoretical philosophy.'

'I don't have it with me,' he answered, 'and mine is small. I'm not so far advanced.'

'But you know something about mechanical science?'

'No,' he replied.

'You don't have any science books either?'

'I have some on natural science and physics,' he said.

'Ah,' I said, 'I'm looking for one on natural science. If you let me have it, I'll pay you.'

The seminarian turned to his black bag, and I was hoping he'd pull the natural-science book out straightaway. But he had no books, and instead he produced the elastics to hold up his socks and shirt sleeves.

I had already noticed he had a womanly face, the beautiful face of a girl, on which lay some dark shadows that resembled the shadows of his Montevecchio. He was hesitant and afraid but fought to overcome his fear and tried to look at others without ever losing his shadows. He stretched and folded his arms, glanced at his blue veins, and stared up at the sky as if at a real cloud or a deeper part of heaven, to place his trust in the glory of God.

Over the next few days, he brought me the book on natural science and then, one by one, a dictionary, the book on theoretical philosophy, the physics book, and a book on the life of a saint from the Tarugo, which is another river that starts at Fenigli. This saint, Saint Martin of the Walls, was an ambitious master builder who wanted to build walls so high that they would reach heaven. His ambition was great but one day, as he was building a church, he couldn't make one brick stand on another until he knelt and sought the blessing of the Holy Spirit.

The seminarian told me that I too had to learn from Saint Martin and not to think I could build my ideas about machines by myself, without the help of the Holy Spirit. But I didn't offend him with the answers he deserved, for I discovered that sometimes, after some strong words I had inadvertently used, he would grow more stubborn and clam up inside his own shadows. Finally, when that September month of my nineteenth year was about to end, he came to visit me for the last time because he had to go back to the seminary, and he brought a box of compasses for designing machines and a special prayer for students to say to Saint Joseph of Copertino.

Next winter, with help from Liborio's dictionary, his book on natural science, and his textbooks, I began to order my thoughts and to write a few pages of the treatise. From my window, I watched the snow that banked up on the trees, on the roofs of the pigsties, and watched how the dog in its kennel grew bored, stretching one leg behind the other, mechanically. Who could have invented the dog, and built the dog with that basic mechanism while equipping it with the organs that humans also have? Mustn't it have been one who was trying to produce a machine and was meanwhile experimenting, working on designs, carrying out smaller projects for experience, to figure out how to get to building the most ambitious machine he could imagine?

I watched the sparrows fluttering on the window ledge and thought what a simple life they led, and I drew that life out as a straight line. I used Liborio's compasses but wasn't yet sure how to keep the drop of ink firmly on the point. I often gave up on the compasses and drew with a pencil. I copied the illustrations in the science book, from stones to the limbs of animals and humans. I could always see their mechanical quality, whether they were wings or arms, and always saw how they were attached by way of a simple moving joint, like the arms of the compasses. I stood the compasses on the table and stuck a potato on top. On it I drew the eyes, the nose, and the mouth of my creature.

Meanwhile I studied words and ordered them according to sound: culture, cultured, cultivated, cultivate, continue, contain; automobile, automaton, author, automatic; genius, genial, genital, generate; and I understood how words together are articulated according to their syllables and according to their sound in a way that was already a construction, a construction that became self-contained, which didn't need to be sustained by my thought and yet was a thought in itself by reason of its force as well as by its design and by its structures, and therefore became something with meaning, and new, beyond the meaning that each word had had before.

After these studies, I could work better and more naturally—running the storehouse in good time and efficiently, cleaning out the cattle shed and feeding all the animals. I went up to the animals and studied their shapes, their individual features. I kicked the sow and knew she would respond with a grunt but, above all, that she would turn her head away from the side on which I had hit her.

In the storehouses where there was no grain, I liked to build figures using planks: fixing them together, propping them against each other, lifting them onto grape crates and broken chairs. I made constructions that had a skeletal appearance, the skeleton of a possible machine. I often tied the different parts with ropes from the beams and left lengths of rope between one and the other and left other lengths dangling. I used a pair of scales for one of these constructions and a funnel for another, a chair for another, or a honey extractor, or a wine bucket. Next day these constructions were different: the balance I had created had altered by itself, and two figures had often joined into one, through weakness or through symbiosis, for one design necessarily complemented the other and this complementary materialism had felt the impetus of its own nature to complete itself or even perfect itself by merging with the other.

So in that winter of my twentieth year, I started writing my treatise. Those four books exhausted me, mainly because their sentences were short and always ended abruptly. There was no logical sequence and no continuous flow, nor, further on, did they reflect that flow of reasoning that sometimes pressed upon my mind. Then I thought of Liborio who, to remember the name of the river, had had to look back at Montevecchio, he with his shadows and the mountain with its shadows.

I had to continue alone, with few resources and few words, and had to force myself not to lapse into devotion, which was also the shortcoming of Liborio's books, before the unity of the Driving Force, the concept of which guided me like a globe. I had to isolate the components of this concept, I had to catalogue them, grade them, and find a rational vehicle that moved and articulated them within the framework that I imagined, that interested me. The movement of this framework, which I found everywhere and whose rhythm vibrated around me, affected all things.

During that fateful winter, in each day and in each thing, there was an alternation of movement and inertia, which tightened around me like a hood—the inertia triggered by a momentary pause in my thoughts, in my observation, and even when the pull of the object, whether a tree or a piece of land, broke the line of movement. This movement and inertia went with the rhythm of the framework I was searching for.

This framework of stars that appeared to me at night appeared like the heart of the mechanism that I had to study and in such a way that I, being surprised by its unity, could make use of it for countless later constructions whose phenomena would connect with time and would be launched into space. The lack of resources left me alone before this space and its time with an anxiety that could have drained me, without the possibility of measuring anything and therefore in the state of seeing that same strip of land that I had harvested being lost, uncontrolled and in the vast expanse and with a thousand possible facets.

I had to map out my research and try to design my framework. I needed books and physical and mechanical instruments and spent much of the day imagining them until I could see them clearly in some place that I didn't recognize but towards which I had to find the way. In my impatience, I became frustrated by the books I had, even by the paper and its print, and I was now afraid they would leave the mark of death on my fingers and some mortal infection, mortal for my studies. Then in February, during Carnival time, when people started moving again between San Savino, Cupello, Fenigli and Frontone for the pig killings and to go dancing, I too resumed the projects that my restlessness was urging me to pursue. Above all, I took long walks so that I could pass in front of Contessa Carsidoni's villa or reach the point at least where I could see the villa. Meanwhile I was curious about the pig killing and offered to help the pig killer, until he let me become his assistant, holding the pig's ears just as he slit its throat and thrust the knife down into its heart.

I always wanted him, and begged him fervently, to throw himself straight onto the beast, to rip it open, so that I could see how life fled from the various limbs, fading away with the last spasms, and to see how death entered and lay heavily on each fibre. But the pig killer said 'no' each time and cursed me. We had to wait each time for the pig to slump with its belly to one side on the ground, then carry it to the tub of boiling water.

Sometimes I had to wake at two in the morning to go and meet the pig killer at the farms over the fields. Often, clutching a stick, I'd cross the fields as far as the roads to Frontone and Acquaviva.

In that coldness, I felt ever more conscious of my body that was pulling itself together after sleep, and I watched my dark feet striding automatically over the ditches and against the breeze and choosing the paths.

On the clearest morning of that winter, around five, clear because of a powdery snow that had fallen the previous evening and which the north wind had kept glistening, I saw two luminous white houses below the horizon where the Megalotti family lived, just as the bus was pulling up beside them.

As I approached, I saw Liborio through the bus window, tall and solitary, dressed only in his black cassock, with a cloth wrapped over his head and his hands together in front of his face, whiter than the frost on the bus window.

Liborio didn't move, didn't turn towards me, didn't see me. I stamped on the ground to attract his attention as the bus was pulling away, but the snow was soft, and I made no sound he could have heard. I couldn't call out for I was short of breath from running and from the surprise, and because my mouth was stopped by the frozen wool of my scarf.

The bus moved off slowly on the snow with its bright-blue cage and Liborio held his head upright almost as if he were instrumental in the journey, or as if to display his indifference like a poor little bird awaiting its fate.

Goodbye Liborio, I called. You imagine you're leaving this countryside behind, but instead you're going somewhere much worse, to a life where your heart is forever locked inside your shameful breast.

Goodbye, I called, and you will see, I'll work for your redemption too.

Calling through my frozen scarf brought a taste to my mouth, and a hunger too, and it occurred to me that had Liborio been free, he and I could have killed and roasted a pig and eaten it at whatever time.

A moment later, I met the pig killer who glinted with his bag of knives.

I began work each day by selecting a knife and examining its blade worn down with use. Then one day my team was sent to kill and joint three pigs for the caretaker, the tenant, and the factor at the villa of Contessa Carsidoni. I arrived at the gate and saw the small avenue where the snow was still clean and untouched like nowhere else in the countryside around. Only on the top of Montevecchio was the snow still so brilliant, where nobody must have gone, and a blue haze could be seen forming over the summit on just a few days of the week, or on top of Monte Petrara above Frontone, where the river rose.

It struck me as a fateful sign, one that placed that stretch of road on a level with other supernatural and celestial places, in the sky above, where my thoughts rose, were enriched, interwoven like my constructions in the storehouse and like the frame that swayed on its ropes.

So not only did I know that this stretch of road, this stretch of avenue to the Contessa's villa, was important, but it was therefore important in the design of those things outside me. I then waited until the pig killer, the factor and all the others had grown drowsy after the food and drink, and I wandered past the animal sheds to peer into the library on the ground floor of the villa. I noted how I could get there again by following the wall and staying clear of the dog kennels, and I worked out a route by which I could climb down from a magnolia and reach the library window without crossing the pure white avenue. But from the magnolia and from the window I would have seen the avenue and its pristine snow shining across my path.

This is what I did and two nights later, with three candles, some matches, and the box of compasses, I was inside the villa, at the bookshelves in the two rooms of the library. I began searching eagerly but on the lower shelves found only magazines, collections of postcards, embroidery patterns, and photograph albums, until I saw the snow of the avenue had begun to grow light and reflect the dawn, with still no trace of any book of interest. I did my best to straighten the library and its collections and left the villa to return home.

I went back each night, fifteen, twenty times, until April. I couldn't take the books away to study them more closely at home and had to flick through them quickly under the candle to find those on science. During the day I found it hard to stay standing, and luckily my work with the pig killer had ended. My father had taken my earnings for himself, so he left me alone if I didn't go down at first light to work in the animal shed or if I slept for a while during the day. I had been depending on that money to order some books advertised in a magazine, books on the occult sciences and on how to build aeroplanes, as well as two on medicine and an encyclopedia of mankind.

And so, having lost the money from the pig killing, on my last entry into the Contessa's library, where I found nothing, not even a science book and not even an atlas, I went through the sitting room up to the first floor and took two silver boxes and a statuette.

The snow on the avenue had almost gone, leaving just a few small patches at the foot of larger trees. It could still be seen in the darkness while I, being sure it was the last time I'd be leaving the villa as a thief, walked along the avenue. The grass of the lawn, as green and tender as one more mirror and one more silk in that house, twisted and turned along the paths, around the fountains and the stone benches, strewn with piles of snow, but also stone and earth. And every so often there was a barrier of green palms tied into one large frond, a maze of foliage and trees like an enchanted garden, where the trees were enchanted and shackled by who-knows-what virtues, and their corresponding vices abandoned, one by one, across the lawn, among the drains, in the shadow. Every so often the ground echoed as my footsteps crossed the carcasses of cisterns.

The night tempted me with its magic to stray from the path of science and to give in to fear. I thought that if I could see through its superficial beauty, I would find in its face the construction charts and curves for all mechanisms. The night had sought to protect herself, but I had crossed her gates.

Before returning home, I wandered through the countryside with not a fear, full of energy, and could feel my strength spreading around me and at the same time keeping itself as warm and cosy as a nest. Spring was dripping everywhere into the darkness and the land was losing its winter rigidity. It was happening all around me as far as the peak of Monte Catria, and in the other direction, towards the dawn, as far as the slopes of Monte Martello. I looked about me as if everything were mine, as if I were a part of it and were one of its motors. The ground softened where I trod, and each step left a deep footprint behind it, open as the sign of something that had been lifted and moved forever.

When I reached the fields and those smoother parts where there were fewer ditches, I found patches still frozen, and bristling vegetation, especially in the ditches, vegetation that was no daughter of that night and whose rigidity seemed like the stalling of a machine.

Those frozen patches were reflected under the faint light of the sky and were silhouetted against the land and the grass like shields or tombstones or, for me, like the flanks of buildings. I picked up a stick and started to flail at the vegetation. I began to form the idea of a connection, like that of a great leap, like that of a great flight along with something real, corporeal, like a piece of a star or a tree, a flight that passed clearly, clearly and simply, through the whole sky and real, then returning to earth, with my ideas as an inventor and my knowledge, holding onto me like the piece of a star. My knowledge gathered spirit and light and shape and colour and substance and sound, like one of the Contessa's boxes, which became as large as a house and rested on the ground as proof of the natural order of machinery, or as large as the factory in which I could enter and start designing and building, so sure was I about what it took, about those instruments and that same certainty that the box instilled in me. And through my design, I could assemble the threads of the supermechanism and the superbody. I watched the threads coming down from the elms and from the oaks, the white threads that the night had laid and was still laying and was meanwhile abandoning around me as I advanced, and which fluttered down, some of them brushing my dark tall path with their bright rays that grew ever-more radiant as the light pierced through every cloud and gave the land the first colours of morning.

Before this factory of mine, I felt sure I could prove the rules about the past, about the beginning, the path and destination of what is natural, of all around that seems immobile and is seen as something untouched by our thought, and still untouchable, a realm of our feelings alone.

I felt sure I could prove this by using my ideas and my studies to calculate *the future of what is artificial, of everything that can be made by man* that is immediately identified with what is natural to the past as soon as its purpose has ended, and its body has sunk in among all other remnants.

I saw with what ease I would re-tread my path, like simply walking around a pillar in the opposite direction: *to rediscover the past of what is natural and therefore to calculate the future of what is artificial.*

All I needed to do was question the land and people, as well as animals, to reach the belly of nature and then to build and then watch the falling geometrical figures of cones, rhomboids or whatever other material form, until I found that point, atom, molecule, cell, monad, that original shared point which is the same for everyone—in other words, until I had established and connected the same consequences and similarities that arise among the natural outcomes produced and aspects of the artificial results.

On that April night, my intention was mapped out only in my mind, but already projected through the light of my eyes which met with that of the dawn, with the reflections of threads that still hung from the sky or fell, and with the lines that the landscape was already forming with its reasons and with its substance, advancing around me beneath the light, taking positions in no way casual, in no way trivial, not as wretched as the ideas of men who rested like glorious machines, hidden in the most comfortable places, in their homes and in their beds and in base domesticity. I was awake for them all, and I stated my argument out loud, by a clump of nearby trees that was turning green, rapidly, rapidly merging.

What shall we achieve in the coming years in the field of invention? I now saw the door of my house or, clearer still, the door of the storehouse that belonged to Signor Mordi, the owner of almost all the land I had walked through.

As I reached the corner, just below my house where the hedges, the trees, the dog, the yard are always there waiting for me, I looked up and saw at the top, in the right-hand angle beneath the roof, where the order of windows is lost and the house seems to end abruptly as if one part had been left unfinished in the hurry to complete it or through the stinginess of some landowner or one of his managers bent on reducing the rooms for workers, up there between the storerooms and the attics, I saw my vast little window, my skylight with a pane of pearl-coloured glass which the wind moved like a blind contraption.

Before going inside I went to hide the silver boxes and took only the statuette to my room, for that statue hadn't yet looked at me, and once past the fence of Villa Carsidoni, its dark eyes had seemed to open and the palms of its small hands to move towards the whole countryside, just as the whole of spring was doing; as if it too had been unearthed at that very moment, and it too had come from some source of water and sky, just like spring, and as if it too had grown softer, changing colour along its back and always finding a different gesture each time I passed it from one hand to the other or took it out of my pocket or put it down for a moment or picked it up again or lifted it up towards the light, different not only in those wide eyes and in its palm, but different mechanically, in its living mechanism as if it were a drop of water trapped in a spirit level, or a lens that could swivel here or there, that could change and be changed.

After that night, I had no great urge to leave the house and go wandering around the countryside watching spring or how things were stirring in that mid-April. I could say I was ill and spent much time in the house once I had done the jobs my father had told me to do. Every now and then, I went back to my treatise and wrote a few words, or drew, and my drawings always led me to take long pauses, prompting many thoughts and then choosing a line, drawing a line that left me, straight and fast as an arrow, and always went to the target that I had prepared. And so, of the many structures around, and of the many things that separate the deserts of glass or all the great wall writings, their news great and small, of gold and silver, I could reach the stage of choosing and fixing upon a specific group of words, lines, segments, fragments, metals, points, and sounds: or upon a single sound, to be placed at a distance or after another arch, at the end of the whole new structure, and I could concentrate on this by inventing it but already visualizing it, holding it immobile but knowing exactly how it could have worked. And this also helped to make me feel happier, to free me from the brutal presence of my father, not to smell the aroma of my house and not to notice those wafts of spring breeze that now moved through every room lifting odours and hems that more than one death and more than one servitude had fixed into the corners or into everywhere else.

And so I abandoned that crowd and allowed myself the great benefit of limiting and focusing my thoughts on those themes and objects I had set before me, on their spheres which, apart from their substances, I could clearly define in a precise relationship with my thought and with the exact realization of it. In this way, at last, my reasoning had a well-defined field and exact instruments, and I could proceed as I wished, with great ease, inventing an infinity of conclusions, an infinity of projects and conclusions of every kind, until I could fit everything together, link all these different abstract and physical entities into a single pattern, form, substance, sphere, object—object, if then in the end I wanted there to be an actual object in front of me, a nail head or the corner of a cushion, to encapsulate, to define all of my inquiries.

In this way I did not lapse into boredom, nor did I squander my research, and I not only exercised my logical capacity and my capacity as an inventor but also gained experience through a series of tests that my mind often felt driven to pursue until I reached a result beyond what I had intended, as if having tipped over a bucket of water, I had stood there watching the water flowing and parting into rivulets, trickling down from one floor to another through no purpose or intention of mine, or filling a hole and dripping further still, parting again into so many tiny streams, each perfect and different from the other, and flowing further on and forever, and yet being the same water tipped over by me.

I wrote in my treatise at the end of April, using the last ink in the bottle that was already reduced to a sludge and had all clotted inside the black bottle with its blue label and cork stopper, so that I began to think that since this bottle was thick, the last object of my constructions, the summary object, the final and preliminary point . . . I began to think that my designs and my thought process might have heated its glass, that this was why the rim of the neck had worn, causing it to lose some of its sand so that the ink inside, due to its weak chemistry, might have managed to separate, to free itself and change one of its molecules.

In any event, I wrote using that sludge that was now almost a product of my advancement along the path of science: *In the various successive achievements of species of organic life, it has to be remembered that at the time when, for example, plant life came into being, designers were already aware of the schemes of animal life in more or less scientific terms, or maybe only as a poetic concept, because many examples of the latter are inspired by the former. Herbs and plants therefore had to be able to extract specific substances from the ground which, jointly or separately, could nourish some of the various species of the animal kingdom; other species in this kingdom are carnivores through the need to balance the effects of relentless reproduction and to stop certain species from taking over too vast a space, as well as to obtain maximum energy with the least effort. All the various species of animal life, however, have been used for testing and trying out mechanical organs and senses that ultimately needed to be selected for humans, even if in a greater or lesser form than that of certain species of animals. Before proceeding to design forms of life or actual mechanical organs, it is necessary to obtain the physical and chemical composition of the matter that constitutes them and with which every small part lives, if only in isolation and maybe for just a short while. If some form of life is derived from a decomposing body in the absence of specific circumstances, this means that the process opposite to composition is occurring but also that there were laboratory experiments to establish and test out with simple forms of life what it was necessary to know for more complex forms of more complete organs.*

And after another two pages, I reached the final sentence, which I quote against Friar Salvi and his ignorance, his own ignorance and that unleashed by him: against Friar Salvi and his ignorance that banished me from the church of Serra Sant'Abbondio under the tearful eyes of Massimina, who had understood my triumph and who for this very reason trembled with fear and exposed her white throat under the arrogance of the others. I saw how her throat sobbed and how frightened she was to hear the monk's words which splintered and fell in the church like objects that had no power to pass beyond the windows and reach the light. I walked out to save her embarrassment.

I will now make an analogy, which I want to call the monk analogy:

If an automaton-creator from other worlds were to arrive on Earth and if, without knowing anything about our technology, he tried to understand how the various successive models of machinery in our mech-anical productions had developed, and he finally attributed everything to natural processes instead of artificial problems and solutions, he would be seriously wrong. Likewise, we too are wrong if we believe the same thing about the evolution of organic bodies. What is more, the fact that these have the same composition as inorganic matter tells us only, and clearly for this reason, that these organic bodies were formed using an inorganic raw material.

One day I received a parcel—six books, of which four were about science, one on the life of a saint, and one containing dialogues.

The books had been sent by Liborio and five of them bore the stamps of diocesan and episcopal seminaries.

One was very old, handwritten; another had several maps showing the solar system, with a picture of the meeting of different currents. At the centre of one of these maps—in which the Sun, Earth, and Moon were lined up inside the same blue riverbed—Liborio had drawn two figures on the two banks, his and mine, both looking at the reader: the only likeness was in the eyes.

My figure had a large head and hands raised, while his was long with big feet and his mouth drawn with a single pen stroke.

Over his head was written 'faith' and over mine 'freedom' in what looked like two small bubbles that clung together among the clouds above the rings of the Earth and sky.

Two books were important because they dealt with the question of man and science, with several chapters on the history of research in physics and mathematics and on measurements and experiments. There were pictures of automatons built in the 1700s, though the wings of Vaucanson's poor duck had been contemptuously cancelled out by some priest. It immediately struck me that the priest would have had little to laugh about if Vaucanson had had a chemical substance for building his little duck. Quack, quack, quack, I said in thanks to Liborio, and returned to my studies more determined than before.

When I did my thinking, I shut myself in my room and sometimes, as I worried over the treatise, I pulled out the statuette and began staring at it. After quite some time looking at it, the eyelids began to swell and the pupils beneath lit up and moved about like a pane of glass now that in the universal glimmer the flies had begun to come up from the cattle shed as far as the panes of my window. The mouth of the statuette also broadened and the upper lip swelled like that of a sheep.

One day I took it with me when I went to doze under a tree. I had seen some hawks and other birds circling in the sky over Fenigli, and they had caught my attention and prompted me to go and lay down under the elms on that side towards Fenigli, as if in such a place and in that position I might have managed at last to receive some great revelation—to find a letter written in the sky, or a body or other separate parts in the maize field that was beginning to turn green and blue. In fact, I found nothing because the two hawks left that patch of sky almost immediately with a squawk and because the maize was nothing more than thick grass badly sown, vigorous and luxuriant through the usual laws of springtime.

I returned holding the statuette, my father saw it and came up to me.

'Give it here,' he said.

'I found it in a field,' I replied.

'Give it here, I'll take it to Mordi.'

'You won't,' I answered.

He went to grab it, but I took a step forward and we collided. He gave me the same look that I always remember him giving from at least the time when I realized, and he realized, that he could never push me about.

'If you found it in the field, it belongs to me,' he said.

'No,' I replied. 'I found it in another field.'

'Then it was one of Mordi's fields.'

'No.'

'I'm taking it,' he said but didn't have the courage to raise his hands and waited for me to yield and hand over the statuette.

'Leave it where it is,' I said and thrust it under his eyes, holding it by its feet as if I were about to crack him over the head with it. He flinched.

'You'd better not go to sleep,' he said.

'When I go to sleep you can go looking for the statue even in my belly, but you won't find it. I'll hide it where all those things you haven't got are hidden, all those things that haunt you.'

I had a moment of freedom now that I had quarrelled with my father, and it gave me the chance to sort out some personal matters. I went to fetch the two silver boxes, dressed quickly, and left for

Pergola. I would always find a car on the road at that time of day, or a bus. Most important was to be free, to start following my own plans, to go where I wished, with not a care, like those hawks I had seen earlier.

Someone gave me a lift on his motorcycle—someone who, from the look of his eyes and his neck, must have been afraid of going into town alone. I gripped the saddle and pressed against the man's back. I could feel the difference between us and realized his back was held awkwardly, with infinite suffering and with such a tangle of forces that he could barely keep upright for the weight of that stress and all the lost energy. I looked at the hairs on the back of his neck and felt attracted to that motorcyclist who didn't look back and didn't say a word. He was a farm worker, as was clear from everything, including the way in which the bones of his skull jutted unevenly between one ear and the other. Our difference made me feel confident and whole, but with the awareness of suffering.

If humanity, I thought, if people don't free themselves, if some of them remain suffering aimlessly in the countryside, and don't even understand why, then whose fault is it? The monk at Serra Sant'Abbondio had spoken about martyrdom and resurrection but, sitting behind this man's back, I understood and could also feel that it was fit only for the grave. If there is such a thing as guilt—and there must be, since all people are frightened and afraid of it and tremble over it—then maybe guilt is this same fear, because people don't want to look, people don't want to face it, and maybe it's this same fear that holds them back. They don't look into themselves, they don't stop to look, they don't look at their land and don't look at themselves in the mirror and don't look up in the air to see how opportunities repeat themselves and how something changes, how a thought changes, or a view, or a threat. They don't look into themselves. They use their thought only in the way that those things around them allow—and by those things around them I mean the trees, mountains, rivers, seasons, those things past and natural which have been put there to serve them and yet, through their ignorance, have turned against them to bring them down and make them slaves. Their fear then becomes greater, and they move ever-further away from themselves and from the whole strength of their thought, searching everywhere for a father and mother and at the same time always for some spiritual sign, some torment. And in the end, they yearn to die, pretending to believe they will then rise again more beauteous and complete, with gleaming feet, in some other place. I know that if there are farm workers and that if that man's back was shaped in that way, this is due to a social system that has degenerated over the centuries through the selfishness and idleness of certain people, and this has been made possible because the social system itself was seen as an untouchable edifice and a channel that enables people to parcel out their guilt. What guilt can this back have, I wondered (and I went almost as far as resting my face against his back), when its owner, on this fine day in May and on this level road, under the sun, in the middle of the country-side, cannot see and instantly understand all things, none of which are fortified by mystery?

It is clear therefore—and I will write this in my treatise, at the end, at the point in which I will outline the programme of *the new*

academy of friendship among all modern societies of qualified people—
that there exists no guilt in the human condition or in the human
structure, and this ought to be chanted to the monks much more
loudly than matins. It is true, however—and I will write this in my
treatise at the point in which I will *set out the tabulated and calibrated
schedules* after having described the unity of the driving force—that
there is an inadequacy in the programming of our machines, in
other words, in the tasks that have been assigned to us. We must
therefore be aware of this—but understand how to breathe, and
strive always to try to understand better, since this striving will also
serve to provide. Leaving this principle aside, and returning to the
question of the monk and the others, since I was then in the slip-
stream of that shirt that wafted in front of me, billowing out like a
spectre of weariness and sadness, it can be said—I too can say—
that the sense of guilt is sometimes a sense of insufficiency and
insanctity, for someone who is a child of God ought to be sufficient
and sure and not a victim of injustices, and so happy not to commit
endless injustices against himself. Around us then is this nature
which, rather than being a maidservant, is the most humiliating
mistress, the expression of every limit, as if we had built a house
for ourselves and, having chosen to forget the doors, had ended up
as its prisoner.

I was leaving with the hope of finding so much land elsewhere,
always beneath my feet and always at my disposal, and always an
energy that would allow me to reason to the point of inventing an
image of the land, of myself and of everything around me, above
and below ground, which was different and scientific. And as I

looked at the hill with the cypresses above the last bend before reaching Pergola, I began to count those trees and to see how the lines that departed from their summit found no obstacle in the landscape of the town or on the countryside behind it that led to San Lorenzo in Campo and the Cesano valley, and could therefore disappear into the blue, and into the blue as far as they wished to go. But the cypresses were fixed to the ground, and I was not; and I therefore must not have had a sacred rule like they must have had, and which had to take account of their much-limited reality.

A deep understanding of nature has nothing to do with those same rules of nature, otherwise what remains in front of us, apart from guilt and fear, is a hideous wilderness rather than a happy and radiant plain, a happy invention that accompanies us, sounding and rebounding around us like the sphere of life.

On this certainty and happiness, I thought of the money I would make by selling the two silver boxes, and said goodbye to my companion, arranging a time for us to return. I sold the boxes to a jeweller in the Corso who took me to the back of the shop. He told me he knew they came from the Contessa Carsidoni's villa, and I must therefore have stolen them. He said he'd pay me no less for that reason, in fact he'd pay more, the proper price, so long as I promised to tell no one I had sold them to him and would bring him any other silver or gold object or picture or statue or furniture I managed to take from the villa. And the money he gave me was certainly enough to buy the books I wanted, as well as to make a trip to Rome as soon as I was twenty-one, when I could go there as an independent citizen and with at least the first chapter of my treatise written out in full.

I thought about going to Rome to meet some philosophers and maybe a group of scientists—in Rome, in the middle of a piazza, in any one of its many piazzas, where there were still unmistakable traces of those who had lived there before us, inventors, philosophers or serfs or prophets of various religions, who still had something clear to say that might help me in my reasoning, that might give some other tangible sign for the figure I could build and which I already felt within me in one part at least of its curves and junctures, even if not in every combination, starting from one point or another and comparing them in accordance with my inventions, discoveries, and the flow of the moment. This was how I imagined the city, the triumph of its beauty, and the contact between my innocence and its opulence, as if a part of it, if only the smallest and most marginal part, were still waiting to be built by me.

I put the money in my pockets and felt sure that all would go as I had planned.

The whole town of Pergola spread out beneath me with its small houses and modest yellow palazzi. A few people were standing outside the cafes or under the portico of the court building. I noticed a rivulet of water in the middle of the piazza that spread out to resemble the outline of a shepherd who was carrying a lamb on his shoulders. The shepherd was standing with his head towards me, but his face was not yet formed by the water and hung over the whole piazza, though I could still recognize it. The lamb's snout could already be seen grazing towards the dust where the piazza sloped down to the road in the direction of the market.

I went to buy a dictionary and some rulers, pencils, and an atlas. Behind the counter, I saw a book in a light-blue cover with the title

Manual of Geometry and I bought that too. I walked happily towards the railings above the marketplace, hoping that my friend with the motorcycle would already be waiting below, at the end of the road to Cagli. He was indeed there, sitting on his motorcycle, legs astride, one hand propped against a tree. It was an innocent triangle that rested against another figure, together forming a whole new figure which gave me an inner contentment, for I already felt warmly towards this friend and hoped I could help him.

When I arrived, he told me he could leave straightway but I wanted to take him for a drink at the Caffè Centrale. He was very sad, bitterly sad in a way that surprised and disturbed me, for it did not fit with my intentions. He was so sad that he seemed taller, as if his whole body had grown thinner. I wondered then whether, at the end of everything, a final reckoning might actually be necessary or inevitable, a day when, on a great plain flattened by machines, the automaton-creators would summon us to account for ourselves and then pass judgement. They would ask how our machines had been used and lost—machines that instead might have brought freedom and perfection to the point of becoming true instruments for their creators' intelligence, to the point of achieving freedom that meant a life without relationships and without rules, organized in whatever encounters a person might desire, beyond the mechanics itself, but also in pursuance of such a complete friendship and harmony that would overwhelm the people themselves and cross the boundaries of their separate worlds. My body and the shadow of that friend of mine were a long way from crossing even a stretch only five paces away from that trodden ground of the marketplace.

I realized then that I couldn't expect help from many people for my projects and that my projects could only be furthered through solitude, study, and through my treatise. If I rejected religion, I would have to be alone and remain alone. It was still hard to talk to my friend because his mother had been taken to Pesaro, so I started looking more closely at the town of Pergola, at the balconies above the parapet overlooking the marketplace and River Cesano, with their iron foliage and with their green foliage in pots. This lay securely around me, since the town was almost empty and the market was deserted, between four elder trees above the outlet towards the river.

It wasn't the bustling town it had been the first day I met Massimina. It was hard then to move among the stalls, a few steps behind my mother. I had heard a voice calling, as if I were a child again in the shadow of my mind's eye, reigning miraculously over my day and over all the people around, reigning over the people like someone indifferent, with long eyelashes: children predestined, alternately gloomy and radiant, who can hold their heads high, lifting themselves and everything with them; who inspire youths and inventors and towns and villages—even where these towns and villages are denser and more closely built at the centre or among hills and clay hummocks.

Massimina's voice was calling, and I couldn't hear what it said. That fulsome sound was calling, a sound that would become unmistakable. So much so that I was caught in the circle of its space, and

I turned and saw her smiling with her dark eyes as close together as flies, and moles all around them as far as her upper lip, who laughed with those narrow eyes and parted lips, resting her head framed by all those dark curls against the silk handkerchiefs that hung from a stall. I turned and started to approach her, as if it truly were she who had called. And I asked if she had called me.

It was my first meeting with Massimina. That day, as I walked to Pergola, I had felt the air above to be freer, higher than on any other day, and to breathe it you almost had to follow your nose, head high, compelled to look at the beauty of the blossoms and shapes of clouds that scudded past each other, high above the stage. Walking was easy, even along the shortcut. I jumped over several ditches, clinging to the broom to pull myself up. I had chosen those paths to save time but also to be alone to enjoy the light that shone everywhere and made the earth quiver.

Massimina made no reply, but I felt as if on my stage I were already holding her and looking into her face, still and ready, like a tree.

'If you don't answer,' I said, 'it means you called me.'

'It doesn't,' she said, bowing her head.

'Then it means you have something to tell me.'

'No,' she said, holding her ground, squinting in the sun, her eyes moving like the tiny hands of a watch.

I felt I could complete that movement, certain that I could touch her face, could make her open her mouth, make her laugh and make her walk wherever we wanted without her even noticing the surroundings or recognizing the streets, happy to let her curls bob here and there, to stop, hold out an arm, show me the palms of her hands, move closer with that rush of fragrance in her dress and across her hips.

'Help me choose the silk handkerchief I want to give you,' I said.

Massimina refused, shrinking back, covering her hands, turning away. She moved so far back that she almost fell into the middle of the handkerchiefs on the stall. I followed her around the whole market and saw that she walked wearily, with some great thought, not just in her head. I followed her for the whole day until I saw where she stopped to wait for the bus. I went up to say goodbye and studied her closely to see more clearly what she was doing, what was happening to her, to the one who had captured my mind and my heart forever. I allowed no movements or rejection, no movements other than the unwinding of that tension I myself had caused in her, just and obedient like the course of those spheres in her eyes might be, or the heaving of her shoulders up and down under the weight of breath for all that I had now heaped on her. I couldn't say a word, nor did I want her to speak, because her voice was now the sound of that morning call, now firmly fixed every-where, as far as San Savino, as far as my house, where before I had had to hide below the roof of my room.

'Are you coming back to Pergola on Saturday?' I asked when I saw the bus arrive.

Massimina nodded. As the other women climbed in, I made her wait, holding her by the arm. Then I went and opened the door at the front and let her climb in. The following Saturday I returned to Pergola on a motorcycle and that evening took Massimina back as far as the door of her house.

As I rode on the motorcycle with Massimina behind, I felt as if I had built her myself, a sweet and lively mass of gentleness, with her submissive curves and her elbows and knees that dug confidently into my body. I had built her myself with the most beautiful design for which, without even realizing it, I had been waiting every day of my life, every moment in which my ideas and reality were forming together inside me and were bringing me the peace of mind to look with eyes wide open and with devotion even inside my whole organism, at whatever object. Now I had this creature with me who had appeared where I had been that moment, and she was my first conquest. I rode confident and happy, not noticing the unfamiliar countryside in those parts of Doglio, but from what I did see I felt I had constructed Massimina by taking the more tender parts of those mounds of earth broken at the base by cuttings and quarries, and the whiter inner part from those woods of brambles. I remembered I had always felt uncertain about those parts of Doglio, with their rocky clefts and outcrops steeped with thorny vegetation, for I had often heard it described as a peak with many sanctuaries and hermitages, and a place for pedlars of quack remedies.

Every now and then I left the handlebar and turned to take one of Massimina's hands, to guide it to my jacket, to the tender part below my ribs, where it soon found a comfortable resting place.

I drove up to the pithead wheels of the Bellisio sulphur mine and watched them turning high up, a worthy sight for Massimina and for our quickening love. That place, Bellisio Solfare, had always been the haunt of rebels, where farm workers would take refuge when they turned against their master, or young bachelors back from military service. It was then a fitting place for our love, for rebellion, for that happy force that I and Massimina held within us. But Massimina didn't want to stop, and we motored on towards greener landscapes that already spread before us in the early stillness of Sunday.

I didn't yet know whether Massimina came from mining folk or farmers, though her jerseys and shoes made me think, from the first moment, that they were farmers. And in fact they were, and I saw immediately from the door of the house and where it stood, that they were tenant farmers, smallholders, tied to the priest, where there's a wife who works as his servant, and a child who is the priest's son or destined for the priesthood.

These are the cruellest and most ignorant folk, who think they are rich and have something they need to defend from other tenants and farm labourers. They are folk who revel and take pleasure, take pleasure most of all in their neighbours' misfortunes and spread wicked stories around the whole area like a fertile garden of injustice.

Massimina proved to be of that selfsame breed and in the end got it into her head to move to Rome, to place herself wholly on the side of the others. This was also because the wealth of the priests and landowners at Serra Sant'Abbondio and Frontone was soon gone. And with it went their arrogance, as soon as they realized that their wealth, firstly everyone else's and then their own, was no more than wretchedness and ignorance, wretchedness painted with ignorance just as someone might paint the door of a cattle shed white. It was enough for a servant girl back from Rome to open her mouth, or someone back from France or Belgium, and they no longer knew what to say and the priests would run and shut themselves in their homes.

Then electricity and television came, and the pretence of these masters was totally shattered. I have to say that I was seen as the cause of the scandal and the source of all their ruin. I was regarded as the most harmful, a kind of Judas who had not hanged himself after his betrayal but had continued to go around banging on doors and walking the streets with his head high, still ready to condemn and to work. I never complained about any persecution, nor do I harbour any spirit of revenge. It just pains me that men and women are lost inside the torrents of their ignorance, and if I carry on perfecting and wanting to spread my ideas, it is to free these people too; and I have to say that every time I have started to talk to them or been to visit them, I have always done so with a smile and with peace in my heart and with much fondness that I would carry in my hands in the same way as one might carry a gift.

My father and my mother were the first to leave me, having sold everything on the day they went off to Rome, to Maccarese, after Mordi went bankrupt. And this was the first sign of great ignorance and perpetual mistrust.

After the last elections, when the Christian Democrats won and a few fascist and liberal votes had also appeared, Mordi had come to tell us that order would be restored in rural areas and that tenants would have to go back to work under their masters, by true and just agreement, and they would live comfortably in this way if they wished, but only as soon as their masters were back on their feet.

I told them straight out that their masters were bound to fail because they didn't have the brains to understand that farms should no longer be worked by tenants but by machinery, and farmers should no longer each be cultivating their poor plot of land but should be setting up large cooperatives that could use many machines, and should introduce varied and more profitable forms of agriculture. Farmers, free from toil, could live happily and some could go and work the machines while others could find work in the cities or could study. Mordi stood up and said this went contrary to everything—contrary, first of all, to religion and then to the dead, and it was in the interests of everyone to have tenant farmers to produce the corn and other commodities.

I tried to convince Mordi that things as they stand are not immutable and, with thought and study, the whole way in which corn is grown and harvested can be changed. And I told him he should listen to what I said for his own benefit, and he should break up the farms, turning them all into one single enterprise. And to make him understand, and to explain more clearly, I went on to tell him how his business should be organized, using all the land to the north for pasture to raise cattle, and the hills used for olives and vines, et cetera. Mordi pointed his stick at me and yelled that I was a Bolshevik. And Mordi—who was very ignorant, even if he was the leader of his group in Cagli and with all his fury held people at least three paces away from him in the piazza—went bankrupt all the same . . . and went bankrupt after twice receiving piles of money and loans to be used for agriculture.

My father said he went bankrupt because he had gambled everything away, and the people of San Savino and Cagli said he went bankrupt because his manager didn't know how to do business, especially at the market. I spoke only the truth. I tried to make people realize that Mordi had gone bankrupt because his whole system was completely wrong, as was the way in which people were still living in Cagli and in all the villages and farms around. My father went off to Rome in disgrace, and before he ran off, he sold all he could, leaving me with just the house and a remote field that belonged to me under the terms of my grandfather's will. And this field, among the best in the area, was stolen from me soon after, with the excuse that before the war my grandmother had given it, of her own free will, to the Congregazione di Carità, in a letter written, signed, and delivered to the priest.

The priest had pulled this letter out after I had started talking about my ideas and publicly expressing my thoughts in my commentary on human nature. I had gone to the priest one day to read a passage I had written in my treatise. I had now received the books I ordered and had found an article in *Il Messaggero* from Rome by an English scientist who described how two electronic turtles had been built which could move along by themselves, knowing how to avoid obstacles, and could choose which way to go and even recharge themselves when they realized their battery was running low.

The priest told me to stop all this and do some work, or maybe, if I didn't want to continue working the land, to get a job somewhere else, in Belgium or France. I simply told him that he was a servant of ignorance. He replied that he was a servant of God and the Church, and that I was insulting both with my ideas.

'But don't you understand,' I said with a dose of cunning, 'that the whole of science and the whole of philosophy are moving towards proving materialism, while I, by demonstrating that men have been constructed by other beings, accept and establish the idea of superior beings that exist somewhere else, and the idea that these beings might in the end turn out to be one: namely, that self-same God to which you call yourself a servant?'

He sent me away and I wrote a letter to the bishop enclosing the part of my treatise which says:

In essence, we do none other than perpetuate the law that governs the universe, which requires that something made of organic matter and then organized into an adequate construction must reproduce itself in order to live, and to survive it must reconstruct itself in increasingly evolved forms through the revolution of successive progressive civilizations. Contrary to what has been believed until now, every form of automaton-creator can build a better version of itself, otherwise we would have to think that in our current state, we have no end and therefore no beginning either. We would have to conclude that we are part of an imperfect system, or that everything has been generated by the whim of infinity with no purpose and no immortal destination. This would mean denying the existence of God, or what we call God, because it is only if we accept that the universe is perfect that we can imagine the creator as having been perfect from the beginning, in other words, that the law that governs this system is perfect and that automaton-creators are its administrators. Indeed, this system is so perfect that it exempts its creator from any direct intervention, whereas he is always indirectly present insofar as the administrators have had full freedom of action, but only to serve the law that governs the universe. The automaton-creator can satisfy its function only by faithfully serving such law. Beyond this it will find nothing but self-destruction.

But the bishop took the same view—that I and my ideas had to be immediately destroyed, first by breaking my wife's heart, then by stealing the field from me, then by stirring all the evil minds in the surrounding areas against me. Massimina began to feel ashamed of me, and this was the cruellest trick they could have played on me and on my hopes.

Massimina was innocent and stood by me for over two years before she started to fall for their trickery. She was still innocent, even though she came from those shady parts of Doglio, among the bramble woods that hid the mouths of so many rocky clefts; and innocent even when she moved, when she laughed, and even when she most wanted to show her innocence around her throat, her small breasts, her eyes, closing them and fluttering her eyelashes here and there like a butterfly.

I thought it was just the mischief of a beautiful young girl, her pink brazenness, and I never imagined she might have been hiding or nurturing some hostile thought, some thought that would prompt even greater deceit, to swell my poisoned veins and ruin everything, to trample on everything and not just me, to unite the whole of San Savino, Serra Sant'Abbondio, and Doglio, and then to turn her back on them by running off to Rome with all her curls, and with her eyes which in Rome, maybe in the gardens of Prima Porta, would open wide to expose all her obstinate malice, which she had perhaps begun to generate from the day of her church Confirmation.

I talk about Massimina like this, but I've always loved her and know I love her even today. No one, no lawyer, no judge, nor even friends, have ever noticed, have ever recognized this love I feel for Massimina. They have all looked on me as if I were incapable of love, as if I had no such feelings, as if the whole of me were raised behind my ideas and steeped only in study.

I've always been seen as someone who does nothing but study and invent, as if these feelings of mine were incidental and entirely lost. And yet my love has always been strong for the very reason that I have always been strong in my qualities and my ideas. I couldn't bear to think that Massimina felt ashamed of me; and most of all I couldn't bear her to feel inadequate, for I wanted her to be the most beautiful and intelligent of women. Instead, she began to feel embarrassed, and would nod and wink at the men who were working with me in the field when I spoke about the academy of friendship among peoples and about the importance of science, and they weren't really listening, so she would shrug her shoulders behind my back, and roll her eyes, and shake her head. How could I tolerate such nasty behaviour, such an insidious betrayal, from the person I loved and to whom I had bound my own destiny and from whom I always expected support? A betrayal as wicked as the wicked ideas of those who are enticed into accepting some benefit that is cheap and illusory but for them is as essential as bread or as their own life—trivial but indispensable and therefore irresistible, even with the arguments of freedom and science, as stubborn as the acquiescence of timid folk, as pointless and interminable as a sermon.

When I discovered that Massimina was so bound to the world of misery as to represent it blossoming and thriving because this world wanted to give a complete picture of itself, to establish a system with births, deaths, protocols of its sordid mediocrity, to elevate its inert matter into a flower, even if this flower could never survive and adapt to its environment, then the love within me immediately turned to violent hatred and I felt I had to beat her, punishing her as well as myself. But I have to say that by beating her I wasn't insulting her—not her. I was insulting the stupidity of the world in which her physical being was an accomplice, in other words, the stupidity of servitude and poverty, where bread and life signify and have taken the place of freedom to live and to build, to move, to think, and above all to believe in others.

The witnesses just stood watching, for they had already made up their minds, and were always quick to agree with what anyone else had said—to say that I beat Massimina repeatedly, for no apparent reason, in the fields or in the house, and even at night if she came bothering me when it was my practice to think, or in other words, to waste time. The witnesses repeated these things with the same persistence with which a dog barks even when no one is watching it. And Massimina played the victim, pretending to smile obligingly, for she still had some feelings for me despite all the ill-treatment I had inflicted. I who had deflowered her with my love, entering inside her like into my own life, into her protective warmth; I who had always loved her as if I were nourishing myself, and touching her head, the hollow behind the chords of her neck, to reach the centre of her every instinct and her consciousness.

Why had she appeared so moved and merciful when the monk drove me out of church, so that I watched her eyes follow me past the pews and out of the door like two moist stars, like two instruments that bent and tortured her body to redeem it and carry it from that holy place and from that band of worshippers and raise it towards a truly enlightened faith? Maybe at that moment she thought I was a false rebel, not a scholar and an inventor but a rebel preacher, one of those who then get themselves a flock and, having once grazed it, end up in Rome and hold onto their flock, not needing to graze it any more. Maybe she thought I was a student, a youth with a smooth tongue who hung around bars, who would take her away from Serra Sant'Abbondio, who would just take her dancing, on motorcycle trips to the Furlo Gorge, by car to town festivals. The monk, at least, didn't just bark and was more noble because he was better versed in his role of indignation and because he knew it was a role he had been given to perform for that poor world of farm workers who have to go up and down the lanes, stop, drink, kneel, cut down a tree, tend a sheep, draw water from the well, continue or, always according to their stature, go off into the hills in a grand re-enactment of the Christmas Nativity. The monk would puff himself up like a bag of wind and would open and flap his great sleeves with a blast of cold air so that those kneeling on the steps beneath him had to shut their eyes.

The monk would puff himself up, draw back his bearded chin, open his mouth, and not just his mouth but his whole gullet, his whole throat and stomach down to his belly, to form the great void in which his voice could echo, like in a cavern. The church was not enough for him because it was small, plastered bright blue, even smaller for the pink stripes around the windows and the arches of the altar. In the void of his cavern, having to hold his face slightly upward and his throat back, he would roll his eyes and they seemed in danger of popping out and bouncing between his feet.

You see, when I talk about my love for Massimina, and about Massimina's betrayal, I immediately invent some image, I immediately pull out a card, any card, so as not to suffer. If I now turn over the poor monk's card I'm left with a miserable low card, worth no points, and before I even start thinking, I begin to suffer—or rather, I suffer, because suffering has no beginning. And then I can think, and I think because I cannot help thinking, and I cannot stop beating Massimina, even though I try instead to teach her, to persuade her. But I could not make a pupil out of her, because I was fooling myself, I was convinced she was truly another part of me and didn't have to be talked to like one person to another. Indeed, when I beat her, I felt I was suffering more than she was, as much for the fact that I was beating her as for the beatings. And yet we were not the same thing, and she, after making fun of me with the others and with her money-grubbing family on the slopes of Doglio, pretended to be frightened, and cried in desperation. And after this, worse still, she tried to persuade me, citing the example of her brothers and her cousins who were working or had gone to work in Rome or who served so-and-so to their great benefit. She was no longer an innocent girl afraid of things she didn't understand but someone who had decided those things were no good and had to be abandoned if people were to remain faithful to that squalid notion of living in San Savino or Doglio or, even worse, going to live and work in the houses and market gardens of Rome.

Many times, in the evening, she would sidle up to me and say: 'Why can't you do like the others?' Or, when she thought I was better disposed, after I had made love to her all night, towards dawn she would say: 'Why don't you give it up?' I would feel a pang of sorrow and look towards the pale light that had begun to filter through the windows. Then I would listen to the cockerel crowing and all the hens clucking and then the oxen thudding at the trough, or I would turn to the wall and stare at the linen chest, and would think that I too could end up like that—inert, brainless, there just to be used, misused, by others, treated as if I had not a thought but were just a pair of hands and a mouth. But then, on those mornings, I would get up and enter the absolute order of the room of the house, and of everything else around, and of the whole countryside, as absolute as the order that the night had been, which is cancelled out between night and day in the perfect suspension of every force, in that moment of inertia, when everything waits for the light and warmth to enter, and for the commandment for everything to do what it has to do. At that moment, people also move apart and, little by little, stand immobile in front of the fireplace or move, little by little, towards the windows. Thought must then be resumed, cosseted, tightened like a belt and the word relished like a leaf on the tree of life. Meanwhile, outside, the light broadens and brightens, and everything is slowly identified in its lair, until distrustful shadows enter too. Then everything shakes itself and begins, and another day bounds forth, towards that new time which the night had sought to deny until just a moment earlier. By which I mean, not the night itself but those who use the night to bring fear, to show how everything so often ends, and how everything grows calm and then begins again in the same way, and then everything is the same and always the same, one thing after another, and therefore to show how fear is right, as well as fear's rule of leaving everything as it's found.

I overcame that spell of inertia with an effort that gradually eased and sent me back sooner to my studies, trying, as I examined objects, to form an immediate view upon them and about them. I thought once again about the linen chest, and thought it was the most elementary design for a machine, and that it certainly never had and never would have a thought, and it consisted solely of its substance and its space and its utility and humility. But if I, or someone more skilled and more able, had begun to give a power of thought even to the linen chest, in other words, another possibility and a possibility of its own, unprompted, then the linen chest could also begin to act differently, to exert that mysterious power which is the reality of seeming to have the ability to make choices and to act. This means discovering and then giving and allowing even machines to exercise thought, and then building so many machines in the frenetic flow of invention, machines that might serve us, help us, thrill us, and even surpass us. Otherwise, by continuing to build machines and more and more machines, and always for a purpose controlled by the rules that our society has established around us, these machines will be none other than bestial, in other words, monotonous and inert, unchanging—in other words, stupid and aggressive, with their single movement repeated, dangerous, and the more repetitive the more dangerous, until they become a threat, a threatening mass looming over us until its mechanical bestiality, through its repetition and its insurgence, sweeps us all away. Machines must be restrained and controlled by giving them thought, giving them a well-regulated system, like a well-regulated thought system. And this ambitious undertaking, as the bishop said, is by no means impossible, as the bishop said, even if it is sacrilegious, and this is so true that even the bishop understood it. We have to commit ourselves to exercising human thought to its farthest extent, and in every possible way. We have to build a society in which all thought can be collectively and fearlessly exercised, inspired by the most ingenious inventions that individual thought can produce. All inventions, once discussed and assembled and coordinated, will be none other than science, which itself will at last be the basis for life, and will be life itself.

To achieve this, nothing must be demeaned by the use of anything in an ordinary sense, especially things that are most akin to thought and to invention, such as words—for example, words put together in a statement made against me to establish a fact that never occurred in the way in which the order of those words puts it, implying also a pattern of motives and consequences. If someone employs words forbidden in the way he has used them, then a certain society will never advance beyond the rules and therefore beyond the prohibitions of that society, beyond the prohibitions that society has imposed on itself to hinder the flow of things that bring progress and development. This is why I am already thinking of writing my treatise in a different way, using words in a new sense and not through the meaning they already have in a story that I reject and that I want to go beyond, otherwise at a certain point my treatise would be another testimony and would actually prove that I am a lazy good-for-nothing, a dimwit, a nutcase, a wife beater, and an enemy of priests and of God.

If the treatise is freely written and the words are new, and if I am truly able to write science as science requires, in a way that will therefore be sweeter than poetry, and therefore different for everyone and new for everyone and abundantly liberating for everyone, then I will shake off the image that those poor old servants of poverty have drawn of me, those who have little bread and few words, and everyone will see me as a philosopher and an inventor.

At this point I have to say that frequently, due to the fuss that Massimina used to make, in or out of bed, coming and whispering the same old stories in my ear, and stretching an arm towards me under the pillow or under my jacket, and because love had often led me to think I ought to live only for her, relinquishing every other possibility for myself, remaining simply in love and tying myself to her so long as I saw her beauty and felt as if love were urging me towards her, overwhelming every other feeling of mine,

I was then overcome by many doubts and often pondered, rumi-
nated, and reflected on my conscience and the choice I had made.
I have always tried to ponder—though it interferes with the progress of my ideas and the completion of the treatise—whether I am
what I am because I have been favoured and marked out, or
whether I am a philosopher and an inventor as a result of the effort
I have made since childhood to observe and attempt to understand
and make contact with all things: in other words, whether my
science is a truth that has been granted and revealed to me at some
earlier stage of my life by an automaton-creator who has inter-
ceded, or whether it is the product of my consciousness and my
reasoning, an unhappy product of my rebellion, of the malice and
stupidity of my father and my rebellion against my father, resulting
not only from his malice and stupidity but also from the principle
I adhere to that everything must be an improvement on what came
before. I think it is like this: that my science is the product of my
consciousness and my reasoning, which is now torturing my poor
mind. But even if I were contemplating a truth revealed to me, I
think this would only be the start of my journey, for I would
strengthen my contemplation through reasoning and study, as I have
already done. I want to be a philosopher and not a prophet, and I
want to write a treatise that is real science and therefore real poetry.
This is why I also want to acknowledge that my ideas can be a part
of me and also that I can eventually abandon them or reject them,
whereas if I were no more than the prophet of a truth that has been
revealed to me, I would, in the end, be doing no more than digging
a grave for my truth, as well as for myself—unless the automaton-
creator happened to turn up one day to explain other levels of this

truth, and then some other day to explain the mechanism. In any event, I continue to plan and carry out and further my rebellion and my studies. Don't the others, including Massimina who was with me for so long, believe that one day someone will come to free them? And don't they believe this even though the one who ought to come to free them is already with them and is meanwhile keeping them enslaved? Don't they believe that this person, on a given day, will have to behave differently, and not in the minds of those who wait and with the contribution of such minds, but simply by walking behind a haystack and re-emerging with a different beard?

I have to say that I don't believe simply in machines, and in their arrival, and that they can create a progressive society, whether at the service of man or of themselves. At best, if we stick firmly to the utilitarian idea of machines that serve man, they can once again create a multitude of servants and farm workers who work for authoritarian beings, and these, at best, will have the problem of not getting bored. But even more seriously, they will be concerned about the whole of society coming to a standstill, about protecting them, and that the machines might go beyond a given point and that this given point is moved or altered; and being unable to overcome this anxiety, they will resort to debauchery and deceit, like any society destined to perish through injustice and the inequity of its powers. You can see how men today, especially men in power, are determined to stop still or to design machines that enable them to stop still; to stop to contemplate the countryside, nature, women, to construct fixed points for each of these things and to try to fix each moment, even space, for their own indulgence, with the absurd insistence on not moving, on surrounding themselves with eternity and immobility. I fear that my statuette was made for this purpose: to give the one who owned it the firmly fixed moment of the gaze of a half-female and half-celestial springtime. Today that small statue beside me has become an inspiration, and I see and agree with it that its eyes are gazing at a point that does not exist, a point we will discuss further on. In the meantime, I will end by saying that men are not prepared to take part and follow the exploration of the universe, and that even those who believe in machines see them, I repeat, in this utilitarian sense. I have to say, then, that through this monstrous stupidity, which can unite mankind and machinery, life can actually end up like the life of bees, like Nazi order, like obsessive selection to the point of creating just one mother, and proceeding in accordance only with normal order, going back and forth even if well assisted and well accommodated, under the direction of a single mother with thirteen thousand eyes, plus those on the side, capable of giving birth to three thousand children a day.

I have to say that people—and this is the purpose of my treatise, though not of my whole life—have been built like machines by other beings who, of course, are machines themselves, and that the true fate of mankind is to build other machines that are better than them, machines that can bring mankind to their level and take it ever higher by building better and better machines. This is the great truth, destined to achieve more than men have ever done. I'm not thinking therefore about machine tools, and my thought is in fact philosophical and innovative, therefore scientific, because it is science, in my view, that can provide the answers—or even just ask the right questions—about the direction in which mankind and its universe are moving. So that point must be found in which mankind becomes alive and free, since it is now proven that no single rule governs and organizes mankind and the universe. Learned professors in Frankfurt and Paris say that everything stands alone and the laws governing the phenomena of celestial beings are not valid for the bodies of fundamental atomic particles.

It's not enough therefore to stop and gaze at the stars and to expect an answer from them. I always told Massimina that what she had to say was of no value at all: she should simply depend on me, continue to love me, and stamp out deceit like cockroaches from the house. Instead, she was the queen of cockroaches and went around hiding letters at the bottom of every drawer, beneath her blouses and underwear, notes for letters, and even whole letters with details and allegations against me. Then, after two years, I understood that she, like everyone else, was frightened, truly frightened of poverty; she was afraid that poverty would force her to pull out and sell all her linen, force her to go off looking for daywork, to lose her status of landowner. Then, since the priests had understood this too, they tried to destroy me by taking away my land, feeling sure that poverty, deprivation, and the loss of Massimina would make me bend to their will like a leaf and reduce me in everyone's eyes to the status of a beggar. The priests, who were sure of Massimina's weakness, therefore continued like that, convinced they would force me to emigrate, to go off looking for work in a vineyard on the hills outside Rome with their peasant cousins, or wield a pick in a Belgian mine. Or, worse still, reduce me to selling almanacs at fairgrounds, a drunken beggar, a figure of fun, the convenient rebel against priestly charity; to wander around the fairs singing, getting drunk here and there, railing against the clergy, so that the priests could say exactly who and what those people are who condemn them. My wife would meanwhile be taken into the service of another priest and her weaknesses once again eagerly exposed, inch by inch, by one who knew that the poor beggar was then tramping the lanes around Petrara or Buonconsiglio, his flesh aching all over. I was very patient because I never felt persecuted and never felt any guilt. Nor did I go searching for those letters in Massimina's drawers, nor was I worried about the visits to her family she so often asked to make. I knew all hell broke loose when her brothers heard her recounting the falsehood about her sufferings and that those brothers had to be forcibly restrained at the door of the house. But I have waited quite calmly for so long and have never seen any furious brother arrive from Doglio, armed or unarmed, or with one of those oak clubs he could easily pick up in the woods of Serra Sant'Abbondio or Montevecchio, cutting across the fields to attack me.

I had purchased more ink and more sheets of paper, and was proceeding with my treatise. Back and forth because I often found the pen wouldn't work or the ink was too light for the new thoughts swirling in my mind. And sometimes when I stopped for a moment, maybe with a certain satisfaction over a new idea, and I paused with the pen in the air as I considered how best to approach and resolve this new thought, I would often write a few sweet words or even a song for Massimina with that same pen and that same ink and on those sheets of paper, which I never dared to send her because I didn't want to give her room to imagine I was trying to make amends for the ill-treatment I had inflicted on her, nor did I want to seem to be giving any credence or substance to that ill-treatment. I left these words or songs in the margin of the treatise or sometimes tore out the sheet and threw the paper addressed to Massimina out of the window like a leaf or a message for anyone who wanted to understand. But I couldn't help noticing that not once did Massimina pick up any of them or make any attempt to read them. From that moment she had lost me, and from that moment she had come to hate the written word, as she later demonstrated by refusing any of the letters I sent her in Rome, and she was already on the lookout for some smallholder or caretaker or clerk who would take her to Rome in a Fiat Topolino or for a Sunday stroll in the piazza in a fur-collared coat. But I was still hopeful and had resolved to fight against the poverty they were all trying to thrust upon me, especially since I realized that those with the most responsibility, the most cunning, wanted most of all to cut off my resources, to stop me publishing my treatise, and going to Rome or perhaps even to Frankfurt to argue it.

In my struggle against poverty, I brought a claim for the land the Church wanted to snatch from me. I mortgaged my house to rent other fields—those same fields that my father had sold before he ran off—and to buy some mowing machines, a baler, and a threshing machine that would enable me to work at harvest time.

Massimina was taken by surprise when she saw all those machines in front of the house. But she soon felt proud and for several days she really loved me, so long as the hope remained that we might get rich, or might just have a business, or work as machine operators. The baler and the threshing machine stood in the sun, dilapidated, poorly made and poorly painted: yellowy orange in colour, with such shoddy cast-iron fittings that they seemed likely to fall off, to be left abandoned far away, and that their engines might drop dead in the yard like knackered horses. I suddenly saw them with eyes different from those of Massimina and soon realized they were the most unreliable machines. At Fossombrone, when I had gone to collect them, they seemed different, still in decent working order. But Massimina's eye had once again revealed to me another deception, while she herself had fallen into her usual arrogant stupidity.

'Why is it you won't believe in my machines,' I asked, 'and yet you look at these wrecks as if they were a group of shiny automaton-creators?'

'Oh, poor me!' said Massimina. 'You're the one who brought them here. And as soon as I arrive you start telling me they're wrecks. Anteo dear, I really think you're not all there.'

'No, Massimina, don't start thinking such things,' I said. 'I'm all here, and with some piece extra and by no means wasted, nothing that should disturb you or me or our life together. I'm a whole man, and sane and happy when I'm near to you, and I want to tell everyone out loud, now for the first time, that I'm not mad, because I've never thought of things pointless or dangerous.

Whereas I'd be mad if I claimed, as many do, at least those who hover around you and want to take you away from here and ruin me, if I thought, if I accepted, that what I am not today, what I cannot do today, no one will ever be, and will ever know how to do tomorrow. I swear this to you, Massimina, that I am your man, a man full of vigour and conscience, and with these machines I'll work for you day and night through the season till I go up to harvest at the monastery in October and to mow the meadows of Monte Petrano in November; and I swear to you that in the meantime I'll put aside my treatise and my studies.'

But Massimina turned and ran crying to the house and had now taken the path of pessimism and malice.

'Where did you get the money for these machines?' she asked. 'We'll end up on the street, we'll have to go looking for farm work in Fenigli or Tarugo, I'll have to take a job as a servant at the mine and sell my linen to some pedlar.'

I tried to put my arm around her at the foot of the steps, to make her understand that nothing bad had yet happened.

'Don't worry yourself,' I said. 'The credit notes won't tie us down, I know what I'm doing, this house will be free from mortgage sooner than you realize.'

'Oh, not the house!' she cried. 'With that mortgage, you've already torn down the roof! We have no home. I can't have a child in the middle of a field! Dear God, keep away from me, I can't have a child if I have no home!'

From that evening Massimina closed herself in what had been my room and wanted nothing more to do with me—sexually, I mean. One evening, eight days later, I left with the machines in readiness for the season. I had to fix a route that took me to the other side of Pergola, from San Lorenzo in Campo to Fratterosa and Mondolfo, as I had been banned by the priests and landowners from going to San Savino, Frontone, Fenigli, Acquaviva, Monlione, Montevecchio, and Serra Sant'Abbondio. No one was allowed to reap and thresh with me. I left at night, driving the tractor, with an acetylene lamp behind the motor that cast a ghostly bright light. I was followed by three labourers with little experience: two older men who drank, one of them with half an ear and two fingers missing, a third young and eager but dressed only in trousers and a flimsy shirt that flapped in the midnight breeze making his teeth chatter louder than the chainwheels of the motor.

The young man would have helped me but needed more clothes.

The man I put in charge of the mowing machine betrayed me later, at the court hearing, and did so on purpose because he had first stolen from me. And this is true, as true as that night of my departure without Massimina's love.

It never occurred to me to make up stories or even just words that hadn't first been backed up by reality. And since they were persecuting me, it was easy to say I suffered from the idea of being persecuted. And I also want to say that, as a matter of principle, anyone who feels persecuted is paying for a wrong that isn't his, he is paying for it out of generosity, and since the wrong is not his, he really is being persecuted. And the worst persecution is placing someone in the position of having to admit a wrong he hasn't done, of having to show his generosity in such a wrong way, for in no other way could such generosity be expressed and be accepted by the society that is persecuting him.

After two days we reached San Lorenzo in Campo, and all had gone well so far. I was happy and saw before me the yellow plain of a promised land. The two men were able to do something, and in two days the boy had learned to run the engine, regulate the valves, and oil the rollers and blades of the baler.

At San Lorenzo in Campo, I went to find the first factor who had to take me to the farms owned by Filippini and by Scalcucci. These were said to be well run and I had managed to get them by charging a very low rate. When the factor saw my men, he hummed and hawed as if he wanted to back out, but Signor Filippini, a man of his word, drove me along his avenue of oak trees to the fields. Halfway down he stopped and pointed his stick at a gap in the hedge which led to a vast cornfield that rippled like a basin of water.

'Go, and by this evening we'll see what you've managed to do,' he said.

I drove my machines with great care into the field so they wouldn't hit the oaks or their lower branches. I parked the two reaper-binders and the tractor next to each other. I went to measure up, then returned to the line of machines and gave the signal to go. The boy drove and whistled and cut, while the other two tottered along behind, but did very well all the same. We laboured as hungrily as if that field were a pot of steaming polenta spread out across a table.

All went well, and I was in good spirits and imagined Massimina shut in her room, and enjoyed the thought that her exile would soon be over. Work went very well at Filippini's, and at Scalcucci's too, and the team and I made a good impression, so we could take a much longer route, as far as Mondolfo, returning up through Sant'Ippolito and then through Fossombrone, and at the end of the season we could work in the fields higher up on Monte Paganuccio and Monte Martello. No priest ever stopped us, and we could work away in peace. And as the man in charge, I knew how to keep order, could prevent the two older ones from getting drunk, and could instruct the boy. We were unlucky to lose several good days at Sant'Ippolito, at the bend in River Metauro, when my tractor split a cylinder. We also lost several spokes of the reaper one by one along the rough roads of Monte Paganuccio until a wheel came off, which caused the machine to buckle, splitting its side. So I had to spend much money having these breakdowns mended since I couldn't fix them myself for lack of tools and spare parts.

My philosophy had failed me in these circumstances, for when I took those machines, always thinking of machinery as a design and a thing that changes by its own virtue and transforms itself, I hadn't thought of asking for a proper supply of basic tools and a reasonable quantity of spare parts.

I went back to Massimina around the middle of September and showed her the money I had made, enough to pay off the instalments for that year and with a good margin of profit. But she made no allowance all the same and refused to sleep with me or carry out the duties and pleasures of a good wife, since the mortgage on the house was still not paid off.

Next day the machine operator—the one who would later betray me—came to tell me where he had left the reapers, one in one place and one in another. One had been there more than two months, the other forty days. Not even the mechanics from Cagli, he said, had managed to put them right. He had done very little work but still wanted to be paid until the first of August, which was thirty-two days after he had abandoned the second machine.

Massimina gave me a look of contempt, for this man was making a fool of me, as if it were my gullibility that were to blame for his brazen malice. I, who could hardly kill him, paid him to the very last lira. Then, still under Massimina's watchful eye, I went up to the bedrooms, where people only go to change their clothes at that hour of the day if they're off on a journey or have some important business. And that's what I did. I changed and let her see me sorting all my money in my wallet and my jacket pocket, and then I left.

I went with the tractor, first to Pergola, to a hotel where I knew I could have a girl. I looked at this girl's body with much distaste, thinking of Massimina, and made love to this body with my eyes shut, thinking of Massimina. Next day I went to Fossombrone to pay the last instalment on the machines, and the reapers too, and without arguing. Then I went to Cagli to pay off one instalment of the mortgage, then to pick up the two reapers, one after the other. I found one behind the school in Acquaviva. Children had dismantled most of it, piece by piece, with bits left lying on the grass. The other was behind the cattle shed of a farm belonging to the Congregazione di Carità and looked as if it had been used up to the previous day, with fresh grass between the blades, as if the Congregazione had already decided to take possession of it, as they had done with my grandmother's land.

When I returned, I found the house empty, the doors and windows all closed. There were no clothes out to dry in the vegetable patch, and the pens around the chicken houses were shut. Massimina had left for her house and had abandoned mine with such contempt as to leave it sadder, with its windows all closed, the storehouses and cattle sheds too, making it look long deserted and its walls more desolate. I went inside and found everything silent and sealed; nothing in my way, nothing lying about like a house that is lived in. There was just a glass in the sink as if, once the shutters were closed and everything locked, Massimina had taken a drink of water before she left. I opened the windows and aired the whole house; I could hear the floor tiles sounding under my feet as I trod. It felt like when the house had been visited by death, perhaps because there was no sound other than the glass panes answering to my steps. I reached the bedroom and sat down to take stock of my solitude, to judge it and to see what best I could do. I lay for some time on the bed with all the windows and doors open in that late-summer twilight that slowly turned into song, through the immensity of its clutches of light and the waves of its languor, all the frogs in the ponds and ditches, and then such a blanket of crickets that stretched from my house to the highest points of the hills. The great silence began, which enveloped the sky and returned across the whole celestial vault into my room, into my heart. I felt my wrists pulsating and felt my legs gradually vanish under the sharp, relentless chorus of the frogs and the crickets. I got up and I went to drink from the glass that Massimina had left. Then I returned to the bedroom, looked into the wardrobes, and saw they were still full of Massimina's linen, her wedding trousseau, and felt a deep sadness in front of these open drawers and piles of sheets and towels. But I was sad because I realized Massimina hadn't gone for good; she hadn't gone through some ploy, the complicity of some family member who had come to take her; it wasn't the result of some plan that I could uncover and repeat line by line until it reached some happy ending which might bring back all of Massimina's love, as well as my peace of mind and dignity, which would allow me the time to resume my studies. Instead, that escape had the air of something spontaneous, impulsive, and therefore something even more desperate.

Massimina's despair must have been so great as to leave her sobbing in her family's home, thinking about her belongings here, while my desperation increased at the sight of those things, which instead of being the vehicle for our harmony and our life together, lay there, abandoned, simply reminding me of what I had lost and would still have to lose. I felt a sudden urge to take them all, to load them on a cart, to hitch up the tractor and drive everything back at night to Massimina's house. But I reckoned neither she nor her family would ever understand my purpose: that I had hurried there with those things, urged on by the desire to see her, to make her feel angry and cry when her belongings were returned, and to make her cry and suffer in the hope that such an explosion of emotions might make her love me again, that she might embrace me once more on the top step of her house, in front of her family. Massimina should have said sorry not just because I asked her to do so but because it would have been the noble way of declaring her love and her loyalty, and of showing how her love made me trust her in my arms to such a point that she was prepared to unite her intelligence with mine and help me with all my ambitions for a happy future.

So I gave up the idea of going to her house with the tractor and her belongings and thought it best to wait and see what she would do next, this time with the involvement of her family. I spent most of the night thinking how this business of Massimina's running off also corresponded with an old pattern repeated a thousand times over, and so often repeated that even a girl like her would so quickly do it. Yet she, with her fickleness, would have had to invent some new idea, and this was exactly what I feared, some new twist that could alter everything else in a way that wouldn't be easy for me to control or respond to. If I had wanted a final separation from Massimina, anything new would have had to be fair and beneficial; but precisely because I wanted to have her back, and her love back, I wanted to follow the usual patterns of those love stories that lead to reconciliation and forgiveness and a whole series of assurances higher than wardrobes, at least insofar as they have no purpose. But at that point, I could have started off entirely anew, just as I might have done with the success of my studies and the public recognition of my ideas. With two years of peace and quiet, I could certainly have finished my treatise. In two years, I would have been reconciled and would have loved Massimina, and at the end I could have shown her more than the trust she had placed in me, could have shown her even more than her trust, more than her very imagination, more than the very language of her eyes, of her hands, of her whole body, more than the language of her live, youthful body had ever, even for a moment, been able to imagine or conceive. At the end of those two years, we could have gone to Rome or even to America or Russia, wherever I was called to explain my ideas and to lay down the principles for the construction of the new machines.

I put my trust in the night, at last, hoping that Massimina's new idea might not be so bright as to dazzle me, and might succeed only moderately in altering my plan, binding my affectionate heart even further with another flow of love.

The morning was not much better, though for a while I managed to forget about Massimina and about her running away and began to study the highest point of the various hills, which on that morning was bathed in light, as the possible point for a more thorough examination of the whole landscape and for a measurement of the days up to winter. But this thought was still forming in my mind, and I had managed only to complete and ascertain the first part of it without reaching the conclusion and considering every consequence when I heard the bus drive past and I started thinking of Massimina again. And the day no longer allowed me those pauses and those opportunities for idleness that can happen at its start and its end, when the Earth has not yet lifted its great head to communicate with all things and is still languishing in the liquid glows of morning and evening as if in a bath.

At midday there was no sign of Massimina or her family, nor any message. At around four or five o'clock, having slept for part of the afternoon, I climbed to one of those points that I had picked out in the landscape and went into deep concentration, forgetting even my frantic love for Massimina, so that I could resume that train of thought which had been interrupted during the morning, returning in the hope it would finally be connected to some communication, to some call for me, or a call I might make to one of the automaton-creators. Indeed, as I walked, I felt that my truth, insofar as it was always mine, always created through the exercise of my mind and everything connected with my studies, might have been granted to me by some automaton-creator even in its most elemental form: namely, as a point of departure or an outline. I felt that my mind, since it was made by these automaton-creators, must be familiar to them, at least in all its parts if not in all its possibilities, yet must certainly have a suitable point to receive from them, these automaton-creators, some stimulus if not control over a perfect operation. I then posed the question whether my mind could not only receive but also transmit to and make contact with these automaton-creators, performing operations which, even if not new—at least in terms of result because they would have done no more than establish a relationship conditioned by the limits of the two entities—would have nevertheless established a basis for my truths, recognizable even to those too feeble to understand and then follow the sense of my inventions; to demonstrate in this way to Massimina, and to those who were ganging up around her ready to come here with hostile purposes, that I was right about creation and could therefore also be right about rebirth. In any event, it would have been perfectly apparent that my time had not been wasted, and indeed had been well spent, for me and for all my neighbours, consumed over whole days and months, as far as the sea and farther still, so that everything, even if it were only an hour or a minute or a piece of land, might have a more exact meaning to me and all my neighbours, and might be an element of great courage and thus of great love, instead of that great humiliation that weighed on all of us, and even on all of those who had left these parts or had arrived in these parts, downtrodden, wealthy or not, even landowners, if then it were true that these landowners in their humiliation—daughter of ignorance—had succeeded only in becoming poor or pretending to be poor, which is even worse, and hiding themselves and turning their faces to chew their morsel of food unseen.

The courage also to understand how all the petty cunning of priests and thieves and landowners and their managers, the cunning of tiny worms born into corruption, is none other than the putrefaction of every attempt to bring about change and innovation, in the sense that they are subtle displays of the great mortal desire to leave everything as it is, barely changing appearances, multiplying only their faces and petty results, and resolving to give great significance to such results when these—which are prestige, the savings bank, the government of others, power, et cetera—are nothing but the worst, the most useless and the most corroded joints of the first organism, of the organism in a state halfway between beast and animal: therefore a state even worse than bestial, because what had been the noble aspects of such a bestial state, such as desire, aggression, determination, anger, and contempt, had already degenerated, and could be replaced by animal humility and submissiveness, which were still poorly developed.

All the ambiguity and meanness of those who are happy and proud to have four or five faces, to hide only their incapacity to move and therefore their own desire for death and to hasten the death of others too, keeping all around unchanged, are none other than the mark of inadequacy and lack of true honesty and of the true ability in themselves and what they do. True honesty means always having the same face, the same attitude, the underlying desire to move forward and sweep things away and uphold the power of life which is the task of mankind.

Here I was establishing an important point about my theories which I hadn't yet dealt with in my treatise: the point from which I could move forward with my reasoning, having also established the outlines of the structure and the construction of human machines, thus setting out the initial information in order to surpass such machines with the construction of other more sophisticated ones: moving ahead to construct a moral philosophy for these new machines too. I would later go beyond the rules of naturalism into which I too could fall, getting too carried away in the face of these machines until I was a slave to their rules, just as all people are slaves to the rules of nature, especially those who are many-faced, of whom I spoke earlier, and also Massimina and her confidants.

At the end of the second day, I was satisfied with what I had achieved, which compensated me for all the time I had wasted working behind the threshing machine and the other machines in my attempt to earn money for Massimina, when—in exact accordance with the rules—her confidants were transformed into messengers and came to my door carrying their message, which was not the true message from Massimina's heart. The messengers were one of her brothers (the younger one), one of her uncles (the wealthier one), and another one whom I didn't know, a go-between recommended by the parish priest and pulled out from the clefts of Doglio as if from a tomb. The three looked anxious and stopped a good fifteen paces from the front door. The brother called, and I let him call three times. When I came outside, the uncle started talking straightaway, raising his hands towards the two beside him.

'We've come in the interests of our relation, to protect her according to the law and put an end to all the gossip. We want to know what your intentions are.'

I invited them inside for a drink but they refused.

'You're right to protect Massimina,' I said, 'and if you were generous and sincere, then you'd protect her as I would protect her, but certainly no better. I know what to protect her from. You don't. And you protect her from something that doesn't exist, which exists only in the wicked customs and ways of this society. These are the customs and ways that can corrupt and offend Massimina, but since you are representatives of this society which accepts these customs and ways, you are therefore the ones who bring harm to Massimina. It is I who must therefore protect and defend her, I who still declares my love for her, and who loves her, and declares that I am ready to forgive her if she comes back to me with humility and trust.'

The third one then spoke, the go-between from Doglio, who began with the very same puff of breath with which the priest had raised him from the tomb and put him on his feet.

'We're here for justice more than protection,' he said, continuing, 'Your ideas are somewhat confused, for we are Massimina's true protectors, chosen by her and by her family. We know you've ill-treated that poor girl many times, in every way, even with cruel beatings, and above all you have deceived her by not supporting her, depriving her of that property, and of the peace of mind you promised her that day when you married her before God. But leaving past conduct aside, we want to know what your intentions are, what you intend to do about Massimina, yourself, your house. We want to know because, if we had to make a decision based on your past behaviour and if you say you intend to behave as you've done in the past, then we as true protectors of Massimina and guardians of morality, and above all as defenders of justice, would have to tell you straightaway that Massimina will be leaving you, that she wants her belongings returned, as well as the wedding ring she gave you—and she wants them returned in good order, though unfortunately her wedding ring can't be returned as it was.'

I was puzzled by this speech, and by such hostile words, especially since the go-between had claimed to be a protector of morality.

'What's all this about the wedding ring?' I asked.

'If you're as intelligent as you say,' the go-between continued, 'for I too have heard you say as much, and have heard you say it so loudly, alas, and so disrespectfully in the church at Serra . . . if you are so intelligent, then you ought to understand how, with your behaviour now and in the past, you've trampled roughshod over the ring you gave that poor girl. After all the wrongs you've done to Massimina, it's no longer as bright and shiny as it was on the day you took that poor virgin to the altar. I can say, however, that we're not here to judge, and that no one in all honesty has been to the police or the town hall or the lawyers. All we want to know is whether you're prepared to mend your ways.'

'And how?' I asked.

'That's for us to decide,' he replied in a manner that made his words seem tougher than I had expected. 'And our decision will depend on how you behave, on the way you respect your wife, on the work you do, which should be profitable work that brings her peace of mind, in freeing the house from its mortgage in a period of time fixed by law, in good husbandry of the land, in the sanctity of marriage, that the night is not deprived of its sleep, nor is it lost in idly gazing at the cobwebs on the ceiling. You must also let your wife see the money you've earned on the rounds you worked this summer, so that this money can be kept and invested jointly and used to benefit your marriage, so that your union might also be blessed with children. Furthermore, and this is the condition that binds you as a man of good sense, you must abandon your ideas and your fight against religion, against the Church and against those who minister for the Lord. You must confess and make amends for your presumption, for it is presumptuous for someone like you, being no scientist and never having studied, to imagine he can plot the course of the stars and dispute the sanctity of life. This condition is the most important of all, since all others follow from it, for if you relinquish your sad doctrine, the Church, not in recompense for removing some threat but as a simple act of pardon, will assist you, not by returning the field which is no longer yours by will of your ancestor, but by compensating you in some other way: allowing you to work its fields, offering many other fine opportunities to encourage and improve your abilities.'

I shuddered and heard at last the voice of the enemy of my ideas, that enemy I never thought would or could exist, that enemy I had always considered to be some invention by those who might have some reason to oppose my ideas, those people who wanted to stop me. But I never thought they could ever really become my enemies and elect a leader and establish a charter and tie a noose with which to hang me, for it was worse to expect me to relinquish my ideas in that way, as if they were a heinous sin, than it would have been to hang me.

Stunned as I was before this enemy, I answered only that I could never abandon my ideas. They were my life, my own self, and I couldn't therefore voluntarily abandon my life or my self.

'These are arguments you might well forget if you let yourself be guided by the advice I have given, the advice I could give,' the enemy said. 'Then you might once again be yourself, and have Massimina, and the fruits of life on this earth. I won't now take your final answer. We wanted merely to give you notice. You have time to decide. But I'll tell you now, both as a warning and as friendly advice, if you keep on this path to ruin then soon, very soon, you'll succeed in losing yourself and all you possess, Massimina most of all. At that point she would ask for an immediate separation, to end the marriage legally and financially, to be sure of her own entitlements, what belongs to her, her furniture, her work, and above all her youth, so they wouldn't be swept away by your ruin. She'll find recompense in some way, in God and in her family, while you will be alone forever, and the whole of Rome won't be enough company for you. I ask you not to give an answer now, for if there were more rebellious words, I'd have to take note of them, however reluctantly, even if they were said in anger. And I'd be worried even if they were words of consent, for they would show an obedience that seemed too swift and too poorly founded or, indeed, worse still, words you would later retract. Say nothing, keep your peace. Think about it, then let Massimina's brother Callisto know in writing. Meanwhile, I'll warn you not to go looking for Massimina, not to meet her or confuse her with words, and even less to insult her with further threats and ill-treatment. I can tell you that Massimina is not at home. She's a long way from anywhere you're likely to visit around here. We'll say goodbye now, and just to show that we leave you in peace and with none of that hostility you have shown, since you've already raised your fist, we'll gladly accept a glass of your wine before saying goodbye and returning on our way.'

I took them to the cellar, opening both doors as if to show that anyone else was welcome too, to show that all those foolish and wicked souls of San Savino and nearby parishes, any who had been or might be led astray by my enemy's words, could come in too.

This man roused no feeling of anger or contempt. I studied his outline and could see only part of it. Propping himself against the cellar wall, to one side of the door, in the shadow, he almost disappeared, and all I could see were the tips of his shoes and the bones of his hands. I heard the noise of his throat gulping down the wine, as if, as he drank, he was shedding the burden of what he had had to say.

I offered them some white wine from the bottom of a demijohn my father had been particularly proud of, using three glasses that were kept on the barrels for those who came to test the wine. I asked to be excused from drinking with them. It was not through any feeling of resentment or betrayal but because I wasn't well. Indeed, I felt a great weakness, a melting from my stomach to my thighs.

The enemy who had spoken emerged from the shadow for another drink and, as he gazed up at the roof beams and the walls of the cellar, asked how much I had mortgaged the house for. He looked like an expert, and I imagined him involved in some way in Massimina and her family's affairs, not through religious or social links as much as some business interest that would bring financial gain. I said I wasn't worried about the mortgage and would certainly repay every lira with three or four years of labour. He smiled, and this time his whole face emerged before me, including the tips of both ears and the crown of his head, as far as the nape of his neck. But the problems of the mortgage, and of Massimina, and of the marriage too were far away, and even if I had wanted to answer to the deputation and its intimidations, I wouldn't have known what to say. I saw the shadows of the cellar and the damp earthen floor that glistened even more. I felt indeed, in this changing moment of the day, that the highest points of the surrounding hillocks were moving and arranging themselves in a circle that might have been crucial. Maybe they were intersecting each other, each lining their summits with the others, establishing a field in which the machines could arrive or be constructed. Or maybe they were establishing a field as a measure I could use to help me understand the whole space of the sky above my house, which had half of its windows shut and half open. I felt that this field was moving for me—for me who, having waited several days, was absent at that moment, busy in the cellar.

The three messengers left. Once past the steps, they turned away from the house, not looking back even at the vegetable plot, not even looking now and then at the fields.

I was alone and went upstairs to my room, to the room where I had slept before my marriage, and where Massimina had gone when she left the marriage bed. I took the statuette and lay down to think. For two days I hadn't eaten, or had eaten very badly, so I thought my illness might be caused by exhaustion. Tiredness encouraged me to think because it opened gaps over which my reasoning was forced to take great leaps. And when, having jumped the gap, it reached the other side, it had changed, had been touched by something, by some acid or by some air current that came from that gap. From those gaps, or maybe from my leaps of thought themselves, I felt a bitter irony over my fate and, at the same time, an urge to push my machine further than it had ever been pushed, to test it, to force it further than ever before while I held it in that position, as it lay, with no pillow beneath its head, down, where the blood rushed and increased the spinning and the depth of the gaps, crowding the patterns of so many thoughts. And many of these patterns did not come from my own body, like all the others before, but I felt they came from outside, that they were caught from the air in that room, which was heavy, with the windows closed and the smell of the fruit that Massimina had left there to ripen. Through the windows I saw only a patch of sky and I saw it silhouetted and billowing like a piece of cloth, like a poor flag. I saw its colour grow and spread, then saw it fade and gradually disappear until I saw the first star emerge, in the very centre of the fabric. Around the middle of the night, when that flag turned bright, after a short while when I must have fallen asleep, I was racked with fever. At night, with the windows closed, there was no sound from outside, other than the rattling panes, at the centre, beneath the point of light of the star. Another sound came from the bed every now and then, when I moved, and expanded the shadow of my thoughts, and pushed it ever further. I felt the fever on my lips, and on my eyes, and thought that I too was sickening like every other being, maybe for the first time, because of what was happening to me, also for the loss of Massimina, which made my house empty, with me in the last room at the top, a gloomy attic.

I kept straining my mind so that my feeling of resentment at the enemy's words would restore my thoughts to a position of trust and devotion towards machines. And so, between one fever and the other, I found myself hoping I might suddenly hear the machines entering that field constructed between the summits of the hillocks, and hoping that these machines were already built and in good working order, and that they had been sent by automaton-creators who had heard about my fate and were sending this machinery to me as a trusty army, as much to prove the truth of my learning as to attack the houses, walls and water tanks of my wicked neighbours and of Massimina's family.

In this anticipation and this admiration of machines, I even lost sight of my supreme commandment to love my neighbours, of brotherhood towards all those of San Savino and other nearby places, of devotion to humanity and, most of all, of trust in the purposes of the universal academy of friendship in a modern society of qualified people.

I kept to my room for two or three days, feeding myself on Massimina's fruit as if in remembrance of her, leaving only for the call of nature, a need that was at first infrequent and hardly bothered me, but which suddenly intensified with such violence that I could hardly leave the lavatory on the outside balcony, until one evening I collapsed exhausted between the balcony and the door. When I came round, I had barely the strength to get up and felt my health at real risk, which was why my ideas had failed to make that progress and produce the results I anticipated. Or else the automaton-creators were close at hand.

I needed help but was certainly too frail for my neighbours to hear my cries. So I dragged myself to my father's bedroom and looked for the double-barrel gun he had left behind. Luckily, there were twenty or so cartridges. Once I had dragged myself back to the balcony on the windward side, towards the houses, I began firing one shot after another, counting to twenty between one shot and the next. People from the neighbouring houses soon came running and I heard voices from behind the thicket. Many were alarmed by the shots while others laughed and joked.

I was carried to the double bed, and I heard them saying there were no sheets when they pulled back the cover to lay me inside, and that Massimina must have taken those too. But I explained that the sheets were in the wardrobe. They left after they had made the bed, saying that they would call the doctor. I heard them shouting and whistling as they went downstairs, and they banged about and kicked all the doors of the house.

The doctor came and treated me. And while I was recovering, Massimina returned. She had only come back, she said before she had even taken off her coat and put down her suitcase, so that no one could accuse her of failing in her wifely duties in my moment of need. Apart from those duties, she said, she was moved also by a sense of Christian charity. I turned away, towards the chest. I was pleased to see her once more, to see her eyes and her body, but I could not thank her for her words, her words that always separated her from every other part of her body, signifying that dwelling inside, beneath her apparent simplicity, was a deep-seated and unmovable conviction about misery, wickedness and the wish to die that she shared with all my poor fellow beings. Indeed, as soon as I was back on my feet, Massimina went off again, I don't know where, just as I didn't know where she had come from. I couldn't stop her, and she ran down the steps like the last of that group of vandals.

I returned to my studies but while recovering my strength, I decided to settle my financial difficulties straightaway by selling the machines. Then I would go to Rome to try my luck in some place in the surrounding countryside as a machine driver, or maybe as a servant or henchman for some powerful person or prince.

Since my studies were progressing slowly due to the obvious difficulties in moving from the first chapter of my treatise to the second—in my attempt to establish a moral code that might give machines a destiny other than mechanical—I strove to improve my draughtsmanship. By drawing I could also examine each object more closely and could understand not only the structure of its various workings but also the mystery of its structure and its whole mechanism. I therefore spent many hours drawing, and when I grew tired of copying, I began drawing from my imagination. But I noticed that I would often fall over, or my compasses or my pencil would drop from my hands while I was in front of things or, on another occasion, as I was quietly studying their reality. This made me feel weak and submissive before them, and indeed weaker than them, and to feel it might have been highly presumptuous to have chosen these as the objects of my study. So the mechanical designs ended up being incomprehensible even to me, with a series of gears that jammed, as if in a pool of water. First, I thought of a pool of water that engulfed them and then, on looking again at the texture of the drawing where the gears ended up welded together, I thought of them welded by solder, all joined and pointlessly buried under a shield.

In moments of tiredness, I put aside the mechanical drawings and started sketching animals. But the tiredness soon returned, and if I drew my neighbour's horse that was grazing by the ditch, I saw that this horse began to fret as if it had been stimulated by the forces that I was losing and that its strength, so much greater, was torturing it and making it chafe and shake its head, flaring its nostrils and eyes, and I could see its strength seething in these nostrils which then slipped and quivered down its neck, to its chest, to the half cups of its muscles, where its hide was softer and smoother and tense with the pounding of its blood.

I was now seized by this strength and, while drawing the horse, I was swept along by it to the point that I made its nostrils flair much more than was natural, and those cups and those rolls of its chest, and its enormous leg kicking, where its strength converged— its leg, which I made as large at least as a mechanical shovel or as the trunk of an oak that reared up menacingly. I was so often amazed by these results and was worried, afraid of cracking up behind them, of losing the sense of my investigations, of therefore losing my confidence and at the same time my health and my sanity. But then I managed to get a grip on the thoughts from which those conclusions had freely developed and to abandon such conclusions and their impressions; I also managed to guide my thoughts honestly back within me and to choose only those thoughts that might be useful. Then I looked at my drawings again, unafraid, and understood they were mere attempts, in which there was always the worry about going beyond appearances and, therefore, about keeping to my path. I could also spend a year or two in Rome, in search of fortune, so that its blindfold might bring success where my merit had failed, or where Massimina had failed, first with her love and then with her bullying, and that of her family and all her friends.

I decided to go to the priest, to ask whether he might need something from Rome or whether he could give me the address of some gentleman who needed a servant.

I didn't want to go to Rome to plough the vineyards on the hills of Frascati or to water chicory in the gardens of Prima Porta or to slake lime at Torpignattara. I'd have preferred to rob a jeweller and, in any event, would have been better off working under the protection of some crooked man of power. I thought, in the end, that by selling the machines I would have quite enough money to make my fortune in some way or other. Perhaps I would settle in Rome and would call Massimina, so that we could share the responsibilities of administering that fortune. Then I could contact scientists and philosophers and could visit the university in December in search of students for my theories.

In the meantime, I kept thinking about writing to Massimina, but stopped at every attempt for fear that this innocent letter of mine would be read by her family. I couldn't therefore talk of love and tell her how much I still loved her and how at night I searched for some trace or some reminder of her or her body. So I gave up the idea of writing, and whatever thought or action or attempt I made was at that moment, at any moment of any day, immediately gripped and tainted by the great open wound inside me, with so many doubts and sorrows; gripped by the thought of that letter I had to write to Callisto in answer to the demands made by her family's ambassadors at my doorstep.

I had decided not to reply, but this decision gave me no peace of mind and indeed it made me worry that it had been governed by hate, for I came to the conclusion, despite the indignation that welled from my body and from its every limb, that my rebellion, and my faith in science, would be better served by responding truly to Callisto with a letter in which I laid out each fact, point by point, explaining the ill-treatment, how I had been tricked out of my money, going with my hands to touch each point in the same hidden heart of those who would read the letter. Then, calmly and openly, I would explain my ideas and illustrate my theories as far as describing the advent of truth.

But such a letter would have been regarded as a provocation and would have resulted in Massimina's family being still more firmly against me. There would have been no chance, then, of being alone with Massimina or of having any direct contact with her. I wandered the fields but every tree, every furrow made me think of the letters I had to write: the letter to Massimina, the letter of sub-mission and surrender, the public statement of my ideas. Each of those leaves still clinging to the trees or falling, not yet dry and shrivelled, was the page on which I would have to write the first words of these letters, and each leaf, beautiful or otherwise, like each blade of grass, sedge, or fern, brought to mind sweet words for the love letter, or precise, strong, weighty words for the public statement of my ideas or, when I saw the leaf that turned in the mud, the falsehood of the letter of surrender.

The land seemed to yield physically to me, to my footsteps, to my gaze, perhaps because of the season or perhaps because of its way of serving and pleasing and smoothing itself for those in power, given that after so many millennia it is now complicitous with those who own it. This land of San Savino, even though it was my land, that of my scientific explorations and discoveries, and which with its limbs had given me a proof or a scientific objective, was now telling me that it would truly be mine and was displaying its fertility, its more sheltered fields, and its softer ditches—most of which would have been mine if I had recanted my ideas by letter under the porticoes of the bishop's palace. This would have been the last road, for at one time I had thought, after much affliction, that I would never write a letter of submission to Massimina's family in which I would have set out my ideas, if only to discredit them, demeaning in that instant every day of my life spent like every scrap of my flesh and every pulsation of my mind. Yet I would have been a thousand times more likely to write such a letter to the diocese, out of respect for those in the halls of the bishop's palace who could read my statement and then frown at my arguments and then be caught by a moment of doubt and could acknowledge my conclusions as a rebellion, and as a noble defeat, but never, as Massimina's families would have done, as a victory for ignorance and as the total and final disposal of a mass of insignificant lurking thoughts that might have threatened their own stupidity and their arrogance. I liked the idea of writing to the diocese, for I felt an urge to end my solitude and instead to fight, even knowing that I would be hurt, to submit to the misery that now gripped me more than the very passion to study and to invent.

My illness had brought me the prolonged company of suffering and I could truly find myself at the point of grieving for myself and starting to accept the notion of being persecuted, and offering my neck to my persecutors, all the more since in that way, at the moment they sank their sword into it, I could have let them discover just how broad and rich it was, and of what precious consistency, and what compelling flow of ideas and blood would spurt out from the open wounds of their cruelty.

Fortunately, I used to go walking and was always making new discoveries, even among those fields where I now caught the sweetness of the last grapes left withering on the vines in the abandoned farms on the hills of Monlione. I recovered my strength therefore by walking and discovering and seeing the empty houses. I felt their languor but also the purpose they had had, and could still have, in giving farmers a free and more prosperous existence, even here at Monlione, if Monlione were turned into a collective farm, a kolkhov, full of machinery, with a new culture, a wealth of geometry and technology, managed by the farmers themselves. And when I thought of the sorrow of those farmers who had gone off to enlist in the army of slaves in Rome, I felt deep down the original, simple awareness—still very small yet certain—of my discoveries. That awareness was the contact I still felt with an automaton-creator and with my research. My research, or rather my solitude, my distrust of my parents and of their world, and of every doctrine that was dished out to me, worse than a bad meal. Yet this awareness, which had remained the same over many years, had been nurtured by my life, and by the reasons I had slowly managed to give to it, and by the truth that it had impressed upon my life and around me. Yet despite everything, many saw me as different, and were against me, and tried to trick me—not only those who could have been brought to justice by that truth of mine which would have condemned their selfishness and their wickedness, but also those ignorant folk, those ignorant neighbours who (if it is true) came to my house during the days when I was sick and couldn't leave my bed, smashed my doors, ripped up my steps, released my pigs and sent them off into the vineyards and maize fields, and knocked over my barrels.

But I still had my strength, and with this I fought against the temptation to surrender to the diocese and to behave like the fields, which were now losing their luxuriant strength and their colour and had commenced their decline towards winter and begun to withdraw within themselves.

Until, as I had expected, the red Sputnik—the machine of liberation—was launched into space, piercing every barrier of hell and of heaven. It shattered the segments of confusion above our heads and forced even farm labourers to look up. It was the true machine of liberation for all, the greatest winged angel that had ever appeared.

Then, in the sudden excitement, I resolved to leave for Rome. In Rome I could make my fortune, and my ideas would triumph, and I could find a group of followers or the protection of someone who, at a single stroke, could give orders to the diocese and send it in full procession to fend off Massimina's family.

I spent the last few days carefully choosing, one by one, among my clothes and everything else in my house, those things I would take to Rome. I could not decide, overwhelmed by my feelings of affection, by my agitation over the flight into space that still fell around me like snow, and already by my feeling of nostalgia for those things I hadn't yet abandoned, over which the bountiful Sputnik had flown. I started putting down on my list even the wardrobes and beds and the chest, even the roof if I could have taken it, or the window of my room, or the bedroom floor with the bricks on which Massimina's feet had echoed. Over the first few days I wrote a long list and then, day by day, I cut it down, until finally I decided not to take anything, except for the clothes I wore, my shoes, a scarf, the statuette, and my money.

Over the following days, I went to sell back the machinery and made three-quarters of what they had cost me a few months before. I took more than half of this sum to pay the mortgage at the Cassa di Risparmio and kept the rest for Rome. That evening I counted out the money, and it seemed little. Then, as it was still early and the dark late-October night seemed favourable, I decided to go and take something from Contessa Carsidoni's villa. I headed towards the cane thicket and the villa, taking the same route as when I was looking for the library. I entered the grounds through the same magnolia and felt assured with each step I took as I dropped down through its branches, as if I were rediscovering myself and the solace of happier days. The black marks of the magnolia on my hands were also comforting and reassuring, and I thought they would help to give me a thief's camouflage, concealing my whiteness so that no one would see me. I entered the villa and started to choose. I

103

went upstairs and found another small silver box but noticed that many things had been removed and much of the furniture was bare. I opened several drawers until I found a gold trinket and some small boxes, and inside one of them some jewels and a garnet necklace as large as my palm and shiny and heavy as a star. I thought immediately of Massimina and put the necklace in my pocket. I looked at the Contessa's pictures and thought that some other time I could take one of those too. Then I left. I climbed through the magnolia without even checking the avenue and entrusted myself once again to the night in the fields and furrows and ditches as far as the top of the hill. Following the same circuitous route I had taken years before, through the marshes of Santa Maria delle Selve to avoid the houses and witnesses, I headed home searching for those silver scudos I had seen the previous time, on that last evening, and which I had amused myself by hitting as a declaration of freedom, and to challenge theirs, and to hear if they had a message.

This time I found some pools of mud and not a glimmer, no metal coins and no sign, no exact correspondence. I found a muddy hunting track and had difficulty reaching the highest hillock behind my house. I was among the canes as if lost, weighed down by the objects I had taken from the Contessa, when at a certain point I disturbed a group of ducks and several snipe. The snipe shrieked once or twice each time they flapped their wings, while the ducks calmed down only when they were clear and safely in the air, their breasts illuminated by the dawn.

I watched the ducks more than the snipe, since those creatures with their long bills were frightened and anxious at any hostile intent and went straight back into the darkness behind another clump of canes, whereas the ducks had flown up high, majestically, and with their calls had settled upon their course.

As I looked for the end of those marshes, I thought how animals too could communicate between themselves and have a shared language and a common intent, even the lost snipe who were calling out in search of their mates.

From the top of the hillock, I could see my house, the strips of vines and the breadth of all the furrows of the land open for sowing in the field that the Church had stolen from me, the land that undulated, as broad as a horse's back, and steamed generously in just the same way.

That day I decided not to sell the Contessa's things in Pergola but in Rome and realized I would therefore need to take a small bag with me. And that was how I left, on the bus for Pergola and Fabriano. That morning, which was still dark, with the objects stashed about me here and there, I admit that I was nervous and felt the scarf tight around my neck. I turned back, opened the door that I had secured with the chain from the well, took off my scarf and tied it around these chains as a fond promise that I would return, that I would remain a free man, that I would never abandon that truth, just as I would never ride roughshod over my own ideas.

I walked down the lane, determined and in good spirit, towards the main road. The pack I was carrying with the Contessa's things was the most suitable luggage to take with me, and for my decisions.

At Pergola, while the bus paused, I had a coffee, then another with a shot of mistrà in it, a double one, and then a small glass of mistrà by itself. At Fabriano station I had another coffee and two mistrà, then climbed on the train for Rome, smoking and content. It was now light, and my homelands were still near and clear yet would soon disappear as if doomed to be abandoned, and as if this fate were in the nature of their rhymes. The train rumbled off from Fabriano and the landscape was already different, with hills and gorges, and vaulted tunnels to receive and conserve the noise of the train. Its windows slammed and rattled back and forth, and the train sped towards Umbria so fast and recklessly that it seemed sure to crash at the bottom of every descent. It didn't even feel like a train going to Rome, nor did the four people sitting around me—all four in a group bundled up and talking, two on one side and two on the other, leaning forward, hands ruddy, listing their things and warning one another to keep an eye on them. I could hear their local accent, not so different from mine, but closer to that of Massimina, and I could hear how they spoke with many an *o* and many a *u*, like Massimina, and how they ended each word by stressing the last syllable with many an *o* and many a *u*, just as those below Doglio towards Umbria and towards the mountains, like in their songs for Good Friday and Christmas, or their pastoral love songs, where even *fiore* and *amore* had a sorrowful note, with the *o*'s and the *u*'s gushing out like blood in torrents of passion. I, though, had my mistrà and tried speaking in order to hear how my voice came out and whether my *o* slipped out through my palate or from my nose with that aroma of mistrà.

'Cheer up, friends,' I said. 'We're off to Rome!'

'Yeh-uu!' all four replied, and they grew more lively after this remark of mine and started talking about what they had done during the festivities, and after sharing each thing they had enjoyed, responded in unison, 'Bell-ooo, bell-ooo!'

'Here's to Saint Romualdo,' I said, 'patron saint of Sassoferrato, bell-ooo!'

'Yeh-uu,' they answered. 'You seem pretty happy yourself,' they added, 'looks like you've had some fortune.'

'Who told you?' I asked. 'It's true, I've had some fortune, though so far this fortune is mine alone, and I'm off to Rome so that I can increase it and share it out with everyone.'

The four didn't understand, or at least not the three men who ended the conversation there. The woman, who was older, was about to say something, but then looked up as if she had lost the thread of what she was about to say, as if it were a strange thought that had taken her by surprise after so long: the memory of a dream or some distant recollection that had come back only to disappear. She looked down at her things, to reassure herself, and ran her fingers over them and settled herself more comfortably under the gaze of the others. They went back to talking about how the harvest had been and what their families who still farmed around Arcevia and Sassoferrato ought to be doing. I listened to what they said. One of them said the sharecroppers and even the landowners were moving away, even from the less abandoned parts where the land was more fertile, since they were still better off in Rome, especially those with land who could open a shop. Five days before, on the train, he said he had met a farmer from Doglio who was going to Rome with a young woman who was crying.

My mistrà suddenly wore off, for I realized the young woman was Massimina.

'What was her name?' I asked the man.

'I don't know, her father never mentioned it.'

'What was his name, or his surname?'

'I don't know. The girl was crying and just said "you, you".'

'Did she have several moles on her face?'

'She did.'

'Lots of moles under her left eye?'

'She did.'

'How was her hair?'

'I don't know, can't remember.'

'Where were they going?'

'To Rome.'

'But what part of Rome? Didn't they say where they were going? To Prima Porta or some other part?'

'No, but the girl talked about some relatives.'

'Don't you remember this girl had a locket around her neck, that her name might have been Massimina, that the house where her relatives lived, when she talked about them, was near Porta Furba? That the girl, when she combed herself, had a white comb?'

The man answered instead with a smile, then said he couldn't even be sure the man and the girl were from Doglio and could only remember—but he was quite sure of this—that when the girl spoke to her father and said 'you', she nodded her head in the direction of the place she had come from and spread her hands and banged her feet too, as if that 'you' meant a whole family or even all the relatives. I stood up.

'This is true,' I said, 'it was her, Massimina, snatched away from me by her father and by her whole family and trying to defend herself.'

'Ah,' said the man, 'but that's not what I said, and I must say it didn't seem the father was dragging her away, for he had no rope and wasn't using his stick. Her father was in a corner, he seemed unhappy, complaining about having to make that journey to Rome, and I have to say, after Foligno the girl stood up, looked about, was curious and started talking to a railwayman, even went into the corridor with him. Thousands of farm workers go to Rome, just like us, from all parts, especially from the Marche, north or south. Don't be so quick to imagine it was your wife the other day. But in Rome, I can say, everything works out, one way or another. You see, if you manage to find her, it's easy to work things out in Rome, you soon forget your village upsets. Or in Rome, once you've seen her, you might lose her again with no harm done, and you go one way and she goes another, on your separate paths, never meeting again for the rest of your life. We're off to Rome, all of us, for less work and more pay, for some comfort too, away from the misery. You'll see, my friend, things will look clearer in Rome.'

'Thank you for all you've told me,' I said, 'but I'm sure that woman the other day was Massimina Meleschi, and I'm pleased,

and anxious to follow her to Rome, to find her once more, and I'll
go looking for her, door by door. This train feels as if it's chasing
after her, that it'll soon catch up. And then, as you say, we really
can forget our village upsets, though I myself don't have any, and
I'm sure I'll be generous enough to embrace her and her family, for
it will bring me pleasure too.'

'That's all well and good,' they said, 'but how will you go finding
her? It's not so easy, you know. It's hard sometimes even with an
address. Tell us your name and where you'll be staying in Rome. If
any of us happens to come across your Massimina one day, we'll let
you know straightway. The four of us live in different parts and we
know the districts and the bars where those from the Marche go.'

'I'm much obliged,' I said. 'My name is Anteo Crocioni, but I
can't say where I'll be, as I don't yet know myself. All I know is that
I'll be at the university in a few days, to talk to some professors, to
show them my projects.'

'There aren't so many Marchigiani at the university,' the man
said, 'and if there are, they'll be porters or property owners whose
wives take in lodgers, people who went to Rome before the war. I
suggest you try taking a tram on Sundays, the red circle then the
black one. Go around the whole of Rome, back and forth, and who
knows, you might see your wife.'

After these words, the four of them pulled out their food and
drink and offered me bread and something to go with it. As they
ate, they quite forgot about my affairs and started talking about
their work and money; about how much people earn per hour, how
much work they do in an hour, how many francs can be made per

hour, and how the lira coins are rounder in Rome; about how money can be lost; bank interest; houses to buy; how much a young woman can earn as a servant; about how people treat money in Rome, and how wonderful to make so much money in a single hour; about how easy it is to do so many hours in a day to earn so much money and how the day is long but not so tiring; about how the whole of Rome consists of nothing more than days of work and money and how much an artichoke costs and how much for a kilo of grapes or a metre of cloth; about how it's worth taking a job in a monastery garden and how employers sometimes think nothing of throwing out things worth a lot of money; about how monks love money or they don't, about how easy it is to catch blackbirds in the monastery gardens and eat them roasted, saving on the butcher; about how expensive wine is but how often you are offered a free glass; about how on Sunday mornings you can clean restaurants or hotels and earn a thousand francs, a thousand lire, so much money, and how you can get a bag of meat trimmings and can use them to make a broth to drink in the evening if you have a snack at midday so as to finish early and get straight back to work; about how, once you've made some money, it's often worth trading in salt or tobacco or opening a bar on the outskirts with a separate room for festivities, but how you need to be careful in choosing which area so as not to end up somewhere that's full of southerners; about how girls should marry shopkeepers rather than employees; about how you can find a place to live even in the centre of Rome, in an old building behind San Cosimato or in Prati, and how people can find jobs for their sons in a government ministry, often through priests or caretakers or porters at a bishop's palace, almost all of them Marchigiani, or domestic servants of government ministers, nearly all Marchigiani too; about how the sun in Rome shines brighter and doesn't have the gloomy face of winter, like where we are; about the risk girls take when they go dancing on Saturdays and Sundays, but how, if they get pregnant, they can get financial help from the Province and then a place to live, with or without the child, through some well-placed official or a legal guardian; about how, once you've made some money, it's better not to go back to buy land or houses in the north or south of the Marche, or in the towns, especially not the towns; about how it's better, if at all, to move towards the coast, to Marotta or Senigallia; about how sometimes, though not always, it's worth allowing children to study, maybe as a doctor; and about how days of rest in Rome can be spent cheaply with friends, avoiding the Roman fixation with the osteria, with eating out, or the cinema, and how instead you can visit churches, which are always very fine and where after certain masses or afternoon blessings, especially if you enter the cloisters and talk to the nuns or the monks or to various priests, they often distribute alms and relics and sometimes even offer accommodation in the convents, or well-paid jobs as caretakers or other chances to work, and always money and permits to enter the Vatican, and in the Vatican you can buy cheap cigarettes as well as sugar, tobacco, coffee, which you can then sell to make extra money; and maybe you can find a small patch of garden in the centre, in the same places where you can catch blackbirds as plump as spring chickens and thrushes too, places you can tidy up, where you can then grow lettuce and other vegetables to sell in the centre, door-to-door, in the local area, at a good price, charging much more, and maybe getting a suit in exchange for a few bunches of lettuce, a pair of shoes for a couple of courgettes; about how money is safe in the Cassa di Risparmio di Macerata, which is one of the best in Italy, and even the Vatican holds money there, and how it's worth investing your money there, even going to the centre, to San Silvestro, to see the city and to post a letter or make a telephone call, and how you must never dare to think of your ten thousand lire as a huge sum of money when you then see that two men in Rome can spend ten thousand lire in a couple of minutes in a bar.

I sat listening to all this as I knew it would be useful to know more about the Marchigiani and to know where to look for them and when and how. I was sorry I hadn't brought a photo of Massimina with me, since my searches would have been easier, much easier, if I could have left the photo with the doorman at the Cassa di Risparmio di Macerata and then be told by him, once he had recognized her, where she lived and even where she worked and how much money—her own at last—she was earning each week or day or hour. Meanwhile I could have gone to the university since, with the money I had, and with the Contessa's jewellery, I didn't need to work and could have pretended to earn at least double what Massimina earned, and double the amount earned by one of her brothers, who would certainly have followed the path that my travel companions had talked about and therefore, even working fourteen hours a day, they would have been earning no more than 1,500 lire a day.

I felt more at ease, especially now that I had the address of the Cassa di Risparmio, and because I could consider how easily I had already thought up the idea of the photo. This would allow me to find Massimina in thirty days, assuming it was true, as those four were saying, that money was best deposited every two weeks to ensure the best interest.

I fell asleep after I had eaten and when I woke the train was already in the Roman countryside, near Orte, behind the meanders of a river that tore its way here and there, as slowly and mindlessly as a strip of cloth. Then I sat gazing at the fields, since the four around me were looking out too, not saying a word, thinking, tapping their fingers on their lips, scratching their hands and their heads. The countryside was empty and certainly not as fertile as the monastery gardens they had talked about. Until we arrived among the houses, around two in the afternoon, with a great sun, and dust in the air, between the houses and the railway, then over the rails and the small railway cottages.

Until the train stopped, and I said goodbye and good luck to my companions, as they told me their names and addresses. But I left immediately as I had no baggage and was eager to see Rome and to be alone, by myself, with Rome before me, with all its streets, the places where Massimina lived or where she had just been or where she might pass that very moment. I almost imagined, in my optimism, that Massimina might leave some luminous trail, like a snail, and that soon I might find her, in that Roman paradise described by the four companions.

Thinking back over those things, I realize what little reason I had to be happy, and how the story about Roman paradise wasn't true, and I can see more and more how much great optimism there must have been, for it occupied all the space of that happiness I had felt. I ought to have kept my optimism for myself and for my studies, rather than for Massimina and my meeting with her. I ought to have been more determined in my studies and more committed to my university projects. Indeed, I ought to have thought most of all about the university and the National Council of Sciences rather than losing myself through my youthfulness, in the circus, and then in my searches for Massimina.

But I also began to worry about money, like all other Marchigiani, when I discovered how much it cost to eat two meals a day in the university student refectory, to buy books on philosophy, mechanics, construction science, et cetera, to publish a few extracts from my treatise and distribute them among university students, to talk to them and offer them a drink in a climate of friendship and, as they would say, of shared research, to advertise in *Il Messaggero* (adverts searching for Massimina, some advertising for pupils for the academy of friendship among people, and some in my search for sponsors for my studies) ... when I saw that my money had almost gone after a few months. Then, having lost much of my optimism, and needing much more to find Massimina, I took a job with the circus in Piazzale Ostiense, as a zoo keeper, which then meant setting up the lions' cage, often in contact with these animals and their jaws, finding them repugnant in the end, having exhausted all curiosity, and with the urge to whip them into action in their cages, to rouse them from their incredible torpor, from their idleness, as an imperfect machine that had one programme alone.

I had joined the circus in the hope of finding Massimina one day when she might have come to watch the show, or might have been passing through Piazzale Ostiense, which is like a great seaport, full of streets, of trams and trains, where people arrive and leave Rome for Ostia, for Naples and the south, where they go to the post office or fire station, or to Testaccio or San Paolo or Garbatella.

But throughout the Christmas period, Massimina never once appeared, for I kept an eye on every seat as I was setting up the lions' cage, disguised behind my jacket. And I stayed there, watching the audience as the lion tamer performed his act, holding his whip, and I would hardly have noticed if the lions had started feasting on the tamer until the meal was over. I had no respect for his courage or his art and was more at ease with the lions than he was, and I entered the cages and kicked them to shift them from their bed of excrement, and while I was watching the rows of seats in the stand, he sometimes leant out in anger from between the bars to give me a half stroke of the whip, but my red jacket protected me, and my contempt and my patience protected me even more.

Massimina had meanwhile become an obsession, and there was nowhere where I thought I might not find her. But Rome was too large and forgetful to remember her, too stupid and mindless, like my lions. One of the customers at the bar where the Marchigiani went, or one the doormen at the Cassa di Risparmio di Macerata, might happen to remember the next day having seen Massimina, or a woman who looked like her, or a woman with many moles, or a woman from Doglio or Serra Sant'Abbondio or San Savino.

I couldn't kick Rome in the way I kicked the lions, so I almost gave up hope.

The professors at the university were just as arrogant as the lion tamer, and as the doormen at the Cassa di Risparmio, and they responded with indifference and wouldn't discuss my publication, or my studies, or even the possibility that they themselves were making use of my inventions, investigating my ideas using those resources placed at their disposal by society itself, which they themselves were now defending from Christian attack. Indeed in Rome, compared with the lion tamer and the Romans, compared with the uniformed doormen at the Cassa di Risparmio di Macerata, they too as surly as the professors at the university and the lion tamer at the circus, I felt like a Christian—in other words, I felt alone, weak, innocent, undernourished, honest, with warm hands, with a great truth, a truth so great that it could not be fathomed by those who hadn't even the energy and enthusiasm to glance at one page as broad as the whole sky.

I felt as Christian as the flesh and the straw that went to the lions, as donkeys sent to the slaughter; as Christian as a sparrow, never as one of those blackbirds I had also seen in the monastery garden or as a pigeon on the great domes or great black-and-white marble churches hollow as death heads; Christian, alone to fend for myself, with a true brotherly spirit, even if brethren were hard to find around here.

I kept Contessa Carsidoni's boxes and statuette hidden in my bed and often looked upon them as my only brethren.

Luckily a nougat stall, the Banca del Torrone, was set up at the circus over Christmas. It belonged to the Burri family, confectioners from Città di Castello, and was run by a father and daughter—the father half-paralysed, the daughter very competent, around thirty-five, quite attractive, though her ankles were red and swollen from hours standing behind the stall, mixing sugar paste. Her name was Elsa. She had lost her fiancé from Città di Castello, a prisoner in Texas during the war.

I used to help Elsa and her father when there were bigger crowds, on the days around Epiphany, and spent much of the time at the stove and selling, so that Elsa could carry on mixing the paste while her half-paralysed father sat most of the time gazing into the air with his head bent slightly to one side behind the stall, over which there was a painted view of Città di Castello and the name of the business. I could easily have settled down with Elsa and could have run the business with her and spent the whole year travelling around Città di Castello and Rome, to the fairs and markets of Gubbio, Foligno, Todi, Spoleto, doing Christmas in Rome and summer on the coast between Fano and Senigallia.

Elsa and her father had a house in Città di Castello, 'all spick and span' she used to say, ready to live in, so spick and span that all they had to do was switch on the lights and light the stove in winter.

Elsa didn't ask about my studies but one evening, as I was switching off the lights and helping her to close up, she asked, as she gazed up at the stars in the vast Roman sky, if I was really sure and knew for certain that those stars moved at great speed, and whether I was sure the Earth revolved, and that man, before being man, had been an animal, like a monkey, or like a fish, if it was true that at one time the whole of the Earth was submerged by seas. I answered yes, where I could, but told Elsa that what mattered was what was coming, not what had been, and that mankind had certainly made progress of a physical kind, which was why it was important to study what it might become or what some of its creations might become, also in its philosophical and moral interest. Elsa listened keenly, then seemed despondent.

'I'll never understand these things,' she said. 'I'm sorry, for I'd like to understand, I'll never understand these things, not because of my religious faith. Maybe it's my life that's at fault, and these four planks of the stall where I've spent it so far. I don't have the courage to look up, to imagine some other fate and revolution for all humanity.'

One evening she said she'd be happy if I remained with her for good. Their season in Rome would end in February when Carnival was over. They'd be moving on to Viterbo, then to Orvieto for Easter.

'Elsa, my dear,' I said, 'I'm married, I love my wife, I'm here in Rome to find her. I don't want to risk making any mistakes, harming you and your father. If I'm in Rome at the end of the year, still in this area, we can see each other. Maybe I'll know how things stand by then, maybe I'll be able to decide better. Don't think that I'm not grateful for your proposal, though I can't answer now, I have to put it after my other projects, projects that are necessary because of other commitments I made before I knew you.'

I wasn't sure I wanted to make confectionery all my life, with little time for study and for my own work, and I certainly couldn't start building a machine with nougat or almonds or candy floss, but I had given my answer.

'At the end of this year, I'll come for sure, I'll tell you something. And if I know sooner, this summer, I'll come looking for you at Senigallia or Fano.'

Meanwhile, I thought, I would go looking for Massimina at Easter, to her home at Serra Sant'Abbondio, or I'd go during the summer, in mid-August, when they celebrate the feast of Sant'Albertino on Monte Catria. And in the meantime, I'd search more thoroughly in Rome once the circus had gone. I had already planned to work full time on my studies from February until Easter, and to make a thorough search for Massimina, helped by my studies.

At the end of February, the circus manager robbed me of a whole month's pay when I told him I wouldn't go with them to Caserta. The lion tamer tried yelling at me, but without a word, I reached towards the handle of the whip, and that was enough.

Once again, I found myself in Rome with almost no money. It was March, the heavens opened, and it rained night and day.

I was in lodgings at Porta Portese, and when I couldn't get on with my studies, I went to watch the Tiber which swelled beneath the rain and raced towards the old port. There I could release my thoughts and give them new impetus. But I couldn't yet formulate an exact answer to the question posed by the professor of philosophy at the University of Rome, namely: In what way, from mechanics conditioned by its nature, with its rules and with its dynamics, could I evolve a super-thought, even by way of new inventions? In other words, in what way could mechanics, having surpassed physics, become philosophy? I had done a series of drawings and once, in a tram, I had almost succeeded in reaching the point, in conceiving the way in which physics becomes grafted and then blossoms as philosophy, when, at that precise moment, I thought I saw Massimina's face reflected in the window. I leapt up but there was no sign of her, and I lost the point I was so close to reaching a moment before.

I was thinking about this point again when I went for a walk, strolling up Via Induno to Viale di Trastevere as far as the Cinema Reale. Much of my money ended up in this cinema, and much more finished up at the pizzerias in Piazza San Cosimato. I hadn't yet tried to sell Contessa Carsidoni's jewellery and my money was running out, partly because I had put 100,000 lire aside and didn't want to touch it until the moment when I had found Massimina and could take her out for a grand celebration, and I could show her I still had money and was optimistic.

On Saturdays and Sundays, seeing that the money was now almost gone, I set myself up on Viale Trastevere, towards Ponte Garibaldi or on the pavement by the cinema, selling lupini beans, or fresh vegetables, or flowers, or marinated olives. I followed the example of another Marchigiano who did the same work all week, who took his supplies from a big woman, also from the Marche, who lived in a large house at the top of Monteverde Nuovo, in some wasteland on the other side of Piazza San Giovanni di Dio.

I often ended up arguing with her as I could never manage to sell the whole basket or the whole tub. Whenever the red circle tram arrived in front of the Cinema Reale, or some other bus that I thought Massimina might be on, I turned my back and covered my bag of lupini beans or my basket so that Massimina wouldn't catch me in such a sad condition.

The Marche woman up at the top of San Giovanni di Dio always shouted at me when I returned, yelling from among the sheets she had hung out under the palm trees in her garden.

The city ended suddenly at two yellow and green apartment blocks, and the countryside began with vegetable plots and cane thickets and a lane that led to this woman's house. The world suddenly changed, and her house looked as if it were in San Savino, and the rows of city housing blocks that could be seen, all alike, in the background seemed like an abandoned stage set, similar to a scene I once happened to see in the garden of Contessa Carsidoni's villa, where members of her family had performed a play and had left a painted backdrop among the trees on which there was a city square with a monument and, on one side, the corner of a building which had the windows of a jeweller's shop and a bar.

The woman would never look in the direction of Rome, and never pointed towards that mountain of yellow houses in the way she might have pointed from her Marche home at a field from which she hoped to reap a fat profit, or at a heap of money, or at an approaching shower of rain that would bring her some good.

'Don't mix yourself up with them folk,' she used to say, 'just sell the stuff. Look them in the eye, don't say anything, and hold out the lupini beans. Don't mix yourself up with them.'

Even though she yelled at me, I began to relax, to feel more at home, more comfortable with her, with those pasta fritters she used to cook for me. She had a son, a clerk at the naval ministry, and a daughter who was married to one of those doctor sons of Marchigiani. They had almost nothing to do with her, never visited, and sent their servants instead to collect fresh eggs and lettuce for their children. The woman didn't want those grandchildren around the house and spent each day making her tubfuls of lupini beans and olives. She must have been very rich, so I thought I might sell her Contessa Carsidoni's jewellery.

'That's why you're not selling lupini beans,' she said, 'if you go around thieving.'

Rather than sending me off to sell, she now kept me at her home preparing the measures for the other sellers and helping her wash out the tubs and carry the sacks. But I now had money, and wanted to return to the university, for in the meantime my studies at this house in the countryside were going well and my head seemed lighter, maybe from the smell of the lupini beans and olives macerating in the salt that came through the doors of the cellar as I passed. The yellow and black tubs and the shade of the cellar all helped to calm my sense of disorientation in Rome and gave me a strength of mind I hadn't felt even in the early stages of my studies.

I told the woman I'd be going back to the university and informed the professor of philosophy on what day I thought I'd be ready to give him an answer. My answer was very simple: I had thought that the heaviness and the limit of mechanics, and the conditioning of its rules, would be overcome from the very start by the intent to give machines moral programming, and that philosophy therefore originated, along with this intent, even before machines. I had also thought that the basis of the programme for the construction of the machines, being deeply moral in its essence, would enable every act and advancement and improvement of machines to occur always in a philosophical sense, and always moving up towards a higher concept.

I was very proud of this conclusion, not least because its evidence enabled me to form a view about an incident that took place at that time, the last thing that happened to me at the lupini woman's house, and because it allowed me to understand how much people lose and how much they are reduced to misery and despondency when they abandon those moral purposes that are certainly the basis on which their machines are constructed, those moral purposes provided without doubt, together with imagination and the abundant fruits of the universe, by automaton-creators to bring harmonious fortune to human machines and their society.

I found myself in the company of thirty or so men who were shocked and frightened by the bullying tactics of the lupini woman's son-in-law, Dottor Colombari. She had sent word that all lupini and olive sellers were to gather at her place, all together, on a particular day to reach an agreement over a collection rota and new prices. When these poor people were all assembled under the palm trees, cap in hand, with attentive looks, Dottor Colombari appeared. After an enthusiastic greeting, he started telling us we should vote Christian Democrat; that the Christian Democrats were working to make Rome great, and us too, with the hope of giving our families and our children a safe future; that Rome was now bright and happy and the Vatican, the Italian Government, and their ministries would work in closer contact for the well-being of their faithful servants, of those who uphold the old noble Christian traditions of the Marche countryside, where family, work, and religion had always provided the most precious foundation.

Dottor Colombari then told them to give their preference vote to his medical colleague, guaranteeing the most considerate care to those in need of it.

'Are you agreed, are you agreed?' he asked. 'And if you're agreed, since you agree, you must support me in this fine campaign, in your interests and the interests of us all.'

The lupini sellers looked hesitant, but they all said yes, all agreed, and the woman, standing behind her son-in-law, grinned because she knew her tyranny had once again ruled the day, and those who gave their vote like this were ever-more tightly bound to her lupini tubs and had yielded once again to her tyranny.

I stared at the thirty lupini sellers in contempt but began, little by little, to understand their humiliation, and as I looked at their tearful rheumy eyes and felt a renewed spirit of kinship, I asked Dottor Colombari what he meant by family, work, and religion, because we may not all agree on the meaning of these three words, we might have different ideas.

The words were what they were, Dottor Colombari said. They were perfectly clear to us all, we all knew perfectly well what family, work and religion meant. The woman grinned even more, and the lupini sellers brightened up too, for it seemed obvious even to them.

So I said, by way of explanation, that family means nothing because each family differs from another, and the family is often a curse, more often than not a responsibility or a worry, and very often the family is an imposition, and that families no longer exist in the cities because they are torn apart by servitude, or they are so divided by other interests that—as they well knew—half of their daughters no longer acknowledged them if they saw them in the street with their lupini tub and their measuring cup. A family, I said, can be of different kinds. It can be a band of ruffians, or it can be well-to-do, which is a different matter, one that is close-knit, ready to defend itself from others, to keep the flame of personal advantage alight. And therefore it's perfectly possible not to know what kind of family it is. This is true all the more with work and religion, which are other impositions and above all instruments of oppression. And we all know what poverty we have left behind us in the Marche, in the villages, because of work and because of religion, for religion is none other than the sad shroud of our dead, and of our own death.

Dottor Colombari was already moving his lips to speak but was beaten to it by the lupini woman.

'You're mad. What you say is nothing but insults. Do you really imagine you can do whatever you like on this earth? You're nothing but dust on this earth, and you'll return to dust before the eyes of these good men, so that I myself can come and trample on you with my own feet. Oh, you think you're frightened of nothing and can live the good life, but I tell you that God will come and punish you faster than you think, for I've seen other rogues like you end up toothless and begging for charity. Oh, you think you can believe and do what you like. You're an ignorant lout. You ignore the good that people want to do for you. But you'll see, you'll find no soil in which to sow your seeds. You'll be struck down sooner or later. You people well know you have to work in order to live. And here in Rome we give you work. This is a place where everyone wants to live, and where you can go by tram rather than having to walk. So listen to those who know what's good for you, and put your future in their hands! And as for you, I'll report you as a thief, for I know you're a thief and can prove it. Meanwhile, you can get out of here. I tell you—in a day or two you'll be wandering behind one of these good men, scavenging for lupini skins to eat.'

'You men know very well how lucky you are,' I said, 'to be in Rome, with no freedom, no education, selling shit on the streets. None of you, none of you have any idea what "government" is, or "ministry", and you tremble whenever you see a tram approach. You're frightened when you see a well-dressed man, whoever he is, you're ready even to let him kick you in the backside, and you'll even thank him for it, just so long as you don't have to talk to him. With your apathy, you even betray the intelligence and the intentions of those who made you, you grovel like worms, you even know this yourselves, and you keep away from the city for fear of your own smell. You no longer even go into your own homes if your daughter has a boyfriend or even just if she's dressing to go out.'

At this point the men started insulting me in a gesture of loyalty to the lupini woman and to Dottor Colombari, and the oldest one hurled a clod of earth that he had picked up, shouting as he stooped to the ground, on that yellow soil, on that patch of ground in front of him, where he was now only fit for burial. The others started attacking me too, though I stood my ground and told them they could heap as much cowardice as they liked upon me. They started pushing me and kicked me several times, but their kicks were empty, and their stomachs were made of parchment.

I grabbed two or three of them by the lapel. 'You poor old men,' I said, 'how I pity you. You won't even get to be buried in your own villages, though you're as good as dead.'

But they started punching me on the back, and one of them struck me in the face with a measuring cup. I hurled myself at them and threw three or four to the ground, and as I clutched those skinny corpses in their fustian jackets, they felt like a single bundle of dry stalks, as if their heads were empty, as if each and all of them had only one of each thing, one essential and irreplaceable part, poor and lost, each part like poverty and perdition itself, each hand or knee or foot, as if it were all no more than the most basic construction kept upright by one worn-out joint, having lost all but its bodily purpose, and as if each body had not been abandoned merely because it was still hidden inside that fustian, because it had those lupini to find, because it still had hair on its head, and because those eyes were not yet completely vacant.

They fought me as if they were rolling about in a pit, as if that contest were a necessary daily chore, like coughing or falling over. They fell and went to get up again, moving further away, brushing off the dust, as if it had all been planned, for they were incapable of thinking that all this was wrong and might have been avoided, but they were forced to do it, entangled once again in their servitude, in some project that was not theirs, which hurled them in like so many dry stalks on a cart. They got up again complaining, since they always complained and, as always, they brushed their clothes down and ran their hands along each hem. In the end, I moved aside.

'There's no point arguing with you,' I said, 'and there's no point even thrashing you one by one. If you want to do some good for yourselves, and since you're nothing but animals, I say you should vote for the Communist Party.'

They stopped and looked around, moving more slowly this time, as if they had detected some odd smell or heard a sound that might affect or involve some part of their bodies, or might harm their clothing.

'Yes, only animals vote Communist,' said the woman. 'I knew you'd eventually stick your nose into that muck.'

'That's right,' I said, 'animals vote Communist, and you know that, and you're sorry. You've always treated these men like animals and, deep down, you're afraid they'll end up behaving like animals. And like animals they'll come and devour everything, even your lupini tubs, since you've brought them up to eat worse than that. Turn your children into doctors, show charity, gather up wealth, give some out from time to time to keep the slaves, but you'll never get over the idea that those around you are animals, that you're a part of God, that you can behave in such a way that people recognize and respect your divinity. These poor dogs have no other path, so they'll give their vote to the Communist Party.

'Who feeds them?' said the woman. 'Who brought them to Rome? Who can send them straight back to the depths of the countryside? Who can look after them, help their children? They know very well who and what can do this. They know who to vote for, who can do this. The Christian Democrat Party. Because everyone in the Christian Democrats works together, united.'

'All right,' I said, 'I'll vote for the Christian Democrats too. And that means that by us all voting Christian Democrat, our vote won't have been a waste of time, for we can all have the same job. Or, if we alone vote Christian Democrat, then I say to you men: go ahead, vote Christian Democrat, even if you'd prefer to vote Communist and if you believe you're different from that woman who goes selling lupini. But if you choose to vote Christian Democrat, joining up with the lupini woman and her son-in-law, then, once you've voted, you ought to have the same rights as them, you ought to demand equal rights. If, on the other hand, you want to vote for power and because you're different from her, and from her son-in-law, because you're frightened and you'd prefer to be back in your villages, hoping your villages might now be different and that in them, in those villages of poor souls, you might find a simpler life and the happiness of your youth, then vote for the Communist Party.'

'Get this madman out of here!' Dottor Colombari said. 'Him and all those lunatics like him who vote Communist, they need their heads examined.'

I said goodbye to my companions. I was sorry to lose them, and sorry I'd had to fight them, not least because that morning I'd been thinking of asking them all to keep an eye out for Massimina on the streets, or asking whether they knew the whereabouts of a girl from Doglio.

I crossed the lupini woman's fields, back to the city. Oh Rome, Rome, how cruel you are, I thought, how pointless you are, with so much land and so many houses.

I took the tram and got off in front of the Cinema Reale, hoping that Massimina might pass on the red circle tram or on trolley bus No. 44. I peered through all the windows and saw thousands of faces, of men and women, but none had Massimina's moles or her complexion, nor could I imagine that any of those women might even be friends of hers.

I peered at the thousands of faces that passed on the circular route, on the trams and trolley buses, and it all seemed pointless— pointless the very way in which the doors of the circle tram opened, and the tram hissed, and people climbed down to the street. I peered at the faces as it grew dark, and realized deep down that the meekest were those thirty poor mummified lupini sellers. I realized they could still have managed a thought, even though they were old. One of those old men might at least have managed a thought, might have absorbed it into his head, shiny as a ruby, between those tufts of tousled hair.

I saw how all those who went past were worried about thoughts, struck by the fear of having thoughts, as if humiliated and worried and anxious about having to deal with such thoughts and having to express them.

In that state of sadness, if I returned to my dormitory overlooking the Porta Portese bridge, and shut the window, and remained there in the darkness and, with my eyes closed, started off from the iron bars and moved forward, and tried to abandon every idea until only my feet and my hands remained, then I no longer had any point in front of me, and as I walked, my hands floundered here and there, I leaned right and left and began to turn until I brushed against one wall and then the other, moving then in an ever-decreasing circle, losing all sense, towards a point that was not mine, but which must have been the mysterious point of my origin, which was still with me, the mouth of the automaton-creator, from which I emerged and which breathed over my machine.

I sat down on the floor and slowly opened my eyes and tried to recognize first my feet and shins. Then I looked for the ray of light that came from the shutter, even if the water from the Tiber at night threw a dark veil out as far as the Aventine Hill. If there was no light, there was still a dark outline that my feet drew in some direction. Then I stood up and decided that I too could go out, could go and see what life there was along the two footpaths by the river.

But this life didn't interest me, for it was the negation of life. It was a tangled spectacle of men and women and youths who did no more than peer at each other, though lost; each doing no more than clutching their chest or fondling their stomach, while someone, from time to time, would wander behind the larger and darker trees or disappear along the steps of the parapet. It was no more than self-indulgence, no more than frenetic self-love: once again the limitation of the machine, namely, the adoration of self and of the machine that can only lead in the end to delusion and loss of awareness. Or else this love, apart from being contemptible, is once again another wish to die, to be buried, to be hidden, and indeed these people on the two banks of the river, even the younger ones, ended up almost always jumping onto the path or dropping behind corners, in fret and dismay, as if suddenly they had found only half of their body.

None of these old stories, in my view, and none of these corrupt practices between human beings can have any purpose in the construction of new days for people and for populations, since these stories and these practices have simply said the same thing, have simply repeated their talk of death, have simply turned their speech around death, pointlessly, as if behind the end of the incidence of life there was nothing else but a vast cemetery filled with every human attempt, with every love and every hope.

Those stories of individuals, just as much as those stories of populations, have had no other meaning, and the same for their customs and their consciousness. And no more has ever been seen, as if beyond death there were the plain pursuit of a human intention, of humans who yet know they can do things, and do these things for themselves and for others too, so they might always improve in their awareness of progress and of its power. It is just as true that even in the perpetual song of death, humans have failed to ignore the start of the programme and have also built a knowledge, even if this knowledge is limited in reality to the search for a series of commodities that might enable people to develop their enjoyment of leisure or even of work, to the contemplation of themselves inside the machine which is always an act of death, and which is the attempt to stop time, to sing their litanies for death with greater devotion. This rudimentary science is what I have to learn and discuss and then try to bring up to date, through invention and the academy of friendship, to turn it into a humble instrument for liberation. For this reason, I must also understand the history of science to see how so many studies and so many inventions have, in the end, been applied by authority in reverse, not allowed to go in the direction in which their force might have taken them, in just the same way that a ball bounces off the wall of a room and is held inside its space.

I wandered among those strangers on the riverbanks, hoping that I might once summon the strength to free them from their idleness and their lust. But these people, on sensing the force of my hope, kept clear of me or gave me looks of ever-greater surprise, furtively hiding their pleasure; or they gritted their teeth, imagining they had something to protect.

But I knew their faults as if they were mine, and felt how the whole city, how every old building or mountain of rags had been built from these faults, and how the river itself flowed between them and how the Roman night was none other than a cover for these faults, inflamed at the edge because something in the air, always, a light or a breeze, rebelled against a complete confidence and abandonment.

Over the next few days, in June, I started going back to the university, for I had to rid myself of Rome's brutality and hoped to receive some confirmation from the professor of philosophy, or at least discuss the conclusion I had reached. But after several days of waiting, this professor sent me away, saying that my research was more scientific in nature, and the only correspondent or correspondents I might find would be among scientists, though not

Italian scientists but Americans or Russians who had more resources and were more advanced in exploring the universe, and more open-minded. He added that he couldn't support or confirm any of my conclusions and felt it better, for the sake of his students, to ask me not to set foot in the university again, for there was no point continuing to argue with his students over matters on which no formal answer could be given. I tried to make him understand the difference between the neat arrangement of formal theories and the long strand on the coil of inventions, but this professor raised his hands and sent me away.

Some of the students I met showed interest, especially those doing physics, but after a while, when our conversations might have become more interesting and when our meetings needed to become more regular, leading to real discussions on arguments put forward by me and investigation of the results, these poor students were compelled, with regret, to withdraw, they too raising their hands, since those in power were calling them back to their work, to the pointless series of repeated tests and exams. I stood at the main entrance alone or waited in the university avenues so that I could walk with some of these students and talk to them as they crossed from one building to the other on their way to the refectory. I even paid for some of their lunches so that they would listen and agree to read what I had written.

In my discouragement, in that solitude and in that heat, I was often minded to think my research was a waste of time or, even if perfect and complete, might remain like one of those small acacia trees that lined the avenues, absolutely still, well trimmed, with no real purpose in that quadrangular university air and in that suffocating heat that seemed, at a certain point, no longer to come from the sun and from the summer, but to be another error of that city of Rome and of that university city and of those people who did not appear and whom I saw only once in the whole day, as they lowered or closed the window blinds.

By the end of July, I was tired and lost the urge to even study at the university library. I started thinking about Massimina again, and with much yearning, and it seemed my studies would only progress and be completed with her beside me, beside me in the summer, in the evening, at San Savino—if she were waiting for me, and watching over me, and only if her footsteps could be heard around the house.

I thought of leaving Rome and returning to San Savino, going to look for Massimina at her house or, if I hadn't the courage to go as far as Doglio or Serra Sant'Abbondio, to wait for her at the festa of Sant'Albertino, under a grove of branches or among the watermelon stalls in the Prato dei Frati.

But the day came when Rome finally emptied its piazzas and its confusion lulled: the day when the professor of physics at the university invited me to his house to hear the explanation of my theories. I arrived among the cypresses and churches of the Aventine, tall and silent as a cemetery, unafraid, sure of what I had to do, with my ideas already on my lips, ordered in so many columns of words, of numbers and of tables.

I didn't stumble in any way, and placed my trust in the professor's clear and empty table on which I knew I could order my thoughts, words, numbers, tables, propositions, and consequences, each beside the other, like an army gathered on the plain.

The professor sat on the other side, with his face over the table like an honest mountain that would play no part but was there to mark the boundary of the plain and to provide reinforcement from behind. I began to explain *the concepts of the unit of the Motorial Being in the five axioms of the first chapter of my treatise, which are the five parts and the five articulations of the framework.*

I then moved on to *the* POWER OF BEING: BRAIN, *with the main chapter of analyses and summaries, and the sub-categories that lie between these two immense conceptual fields and within them.*

I listed the sections:

1. FREE WILL, COMPASS, KNOWLEDGE, ENVIRONMENT, REFLECTION, IMAGINATION: *paramount ordered power unleashed from nothingness; vast prestigious command derived from everything.*

2. WISDOM, CULTURE, VIRTUE, TALENT, MENTALITY: *universal life force imparted from spontaneous pride; innate strength trans-formed from forced courage.*

3. IDEAL, QUALITY, JUDGEMENT, GENIUS, QUANTITY, CRI-TERION: *guide to the efforts assumed by individual species; key to absolute benefits of each genus.*

4. CONSCIOUS MIND UNDERSTANDING, SPIRIT RESPONSE WILL: *intimate and attentive desires; stimulus of matured and prudent passions.*

5. MORALS, MINERALS, FEELINGS, MATTER, IMPULSES: *ethereal measure defined by principles; corporeal testing ground repeated to infinity.*

The professor listened in much the same way that the mountain listens to the plain and comforts or controls it with its silence.

I moved on to the numerical subdivision and continued: *'science, technology of the philosophical mechanism of the organism.'*

I wanted to pass to the nominal subdivision, but the professor asked me to move on to the machine and to be brief. I showed him that two chapters of my treatise were, in fact, called 'Brief and Incidental Comment' and 'Brief and Incidental Approach'. Before passing on to the machine, I said, I first had to explain the IMMENSE SOLIDITIES from which human solidities were derived. I found the largest space on the plain and declared triumphantly, seeing the words forming themselves with courage and conviction like soldiers under orders to defend the ultimate virtue of the mass of humanity and of Mother Earth: *'The moment of creation is conceived as an eternal attribute of the contributions of the origin of the congenital creation of the universe. The workings are therefore explained, and their articulations demonstrated, by contributing to the origin of creation with the first traces of mechanics, which is synonymous with God, even if it were only the mark of an attempt, namely of freedom.'*

At this point I presented the first table, and this table at the far end of the plain constituted a perfect fortification: its constructions formed an impregnable mass, as the absolute proof that might be given by a precocious child when he displays his mud castle to show off his creative skill, believing it to be indestructible and worthy of the everlasting respect of all mankind.

```
        ,                    ;                    .
       YYY                  YYY                  YYY
      YYYYY                YYYYY                YYYYY
     YYYYYYY              YYYYYYY              YYYYYYY
    YYYYYYYYY            YYYYYYYYY            YYYYYYYYY
   YYYYYYYYYYY    !     YYYYYYYYYYY    ?     YYYYYYYYYYY
  YYYYYYYYYYYYY YYY YYYYYYYYYYYYY YYY YYYYYYYYYYYYY
  YYYYYYYYYYYYY YYYYY YYYYYYYYYYY YYYYY YYYYYYYYYYYYY
  YYYYYYYYYYYYY YYYYYYY YYYYYYYYY YYYYYYY YYYYYYYYYYYYY
  YYYYYYYYYYYYY YYYYYYYYY YYYYYYY YYYYYYYYY YYYYYYYYYYYY
  YYYYYYYYYYYYY YYYYYYYYY YYYYYYY YYYYYYYYY YYYYYYYYYYYY


        ,                    ;                    .
       HHH                  HHH                  HHH
      HHHHH                HHHHH                HHHHH
     HHHHHHH              HHHHHHH              HHHHHHH
    HHHHHHHHH            HHHHHHHHH            HHHHHHHHH
   HHHHHHHHHHH    !     HHHHHHHHHHH    ?     HHHHHHHHHHH
  HHHHHHHHHHHHH HHH HHHHHHHHHHHHH HHH HHHHHHHHHHHHH
  HHHHHHHHHHHHH HHHHH HHHHHHHHHHH HHHHH HHHHHHHHHHHHH
  HHHHHHHHHHHHH HHHHHHH HHHHHHHHH HHHHHHH HHHHHHHHHHHHH
  HHHHHHHHHHHHH HHHHHHHHH HHHHHHH HHHHHHHHH HHHHHHHHHHHH
  HHHHHHHHHHHHH HHHHHHHHH HHHHHHH HHHHHHHHH HHHHHHHHHHHH


        ,                    ;                    .
       XXX                  XXX                  XXX
      XXXXX                XXXXX                XXXXX
     XXXXXXX              XXXXXXX              XXXXXXX
    XXXXXXXXX            XXXXXXXXX            XXXXXXXXX
   XXXXXXXXXXX    !     XXXXXXXXXXX    ?     XXXXXXXXXXX
  XXXXXXXXXXXXX XXX XXXXXXXXXXXXX XXX XXXXXXXXXXXXX
  XXXXXXXXXXXXX XXXXX XXXXXXXXXXX XXXXX XXXXXXXXXXXXX
  XXXXXXXXXXXXX XXXXXXX XXXXXXXXX XXXXXXX XXXXXXXXXXXXX
  XXXXXXXXXXXXX XXXXXXXXX XXXXXXX XXXXXXXXX XXXXXXXXXXXX
  XXXXXXXXXXXXX XXXXXXXXX XXXXXXX XXXXXXXXX XXXXXXXXXXXX
```

But the professor looked dismayed.

'Quite frankly,' he said, 'I don't understand. These drawings are very nice, but they don't seem mechanical to me, they seem poetical.'

'Ah!' I said, 'this is the aestheticism that all of you have, which wrestles once again with your own scientific frames of mind.'

'Why?' he asked.

'Because you want to see only the beauty of these constructions and not the scientific rule that keeps them standing; or, if you like, this skeleton here gives a solid indication of the brutality of your society, which is prettified with face powder to become a false beauty, but which is always kept standing by the same form, which is that constant form of dejection and death: of death = X, of contempt = H, of fear = Y.'

'All right,' the professor said, 'I'll think about these matters and let you have an answer, though I have to say that so far, quite frankly, they don't seem very clear to me, and I find their scientific basis somewhat doubtful.'

But he didn't see the plain, and he didn't see the precise columns of all my conceptions as far as the machines, as far as the idea of their dynamism and evolution, as far as the castles of the tables which were illuminated to live eternally on the clear glass of his study.

'One moment,' I said. 'May I present my conclusions? I have some scientific and moral explanations that need to be considered, even just for a minute, in this world that's on the point of ruin.

How could man become so corrupt? Since you yourself cannot explain it, please listen. Accept the privilege of being the only person on this earth to have received my revelations.'

'All right,' the professor said, and ordered the maid to bring in some tea and cakes.

'*In progressive societies which improve life in order to develop existence*,' I began, '*everything happens through the superimposition of new events, given that in no single instance can we know beforehand what can be done later. It is clear, however, that anything, since it is temporary and will eventually die, must come from other temporary phenomena: which is why things are able to improve and develop through daily superimpositions. Evolution is therefore the very essence of the formation of the automaton-creator. This procedure shows us that nothing is eternal in itself and demonstrates how it becomes so by connecting itself to other things in the universe; but that everything happens only if there are automaton-creators supplied with a motor-brain.*'

'This may all be most intuitive,' said the professor, 'but who knows if poetry also embraces physics? How does this concept of evolution stand in physical terms?'

I stood up to give my answer: '*The creative instant, conceived as a dynamic, automatic, psychological and scientific whole, is the origin of creation, activated by the validity of the arguments and authority of the instruments available to automaton-creators. They serve the perpetual needs of creation through their capacity to stir questions and raise possibilities for tackling the problems of progressive civilization, in the steadfast struggle of individuals for the massive conquests of generations.*'

I spent another couple of days in the Porta Portese area and met one of the lupini sellers who told me he had heard that a girl from Doglio was in Rome, in Via Uruguay, and that she was very sad and spent all her spare time sitting in a pine grove near where she lived. I went to Via Uruguay but found no girl from Doglio, not in the market, nor in the shops, nor on Sunday in the pine grove.

There was a police station at the end of the road, so one day I walked in and asked if they knew Massimina Crocioni Meleschi and knew where she lived. They wanted to know why I was asking, and the officer told me in the end that to find Massimina they would need an official complaint. I would have to report my wife for desertion. I went ahead with the complaint in the hope of finding Massimina, convinced that it simply meant that I wanted to find her, and since I couldn't find her myself and didn't know who to turn to, I was asking the police for help, the most simple and honest help, so they could find her and just tell me where she lived. Then, from that moment, I thought they would disappear, happy to have been of service to a citizen and to have helped him out.

After two or three days, the policeman told me that since it was August, no one was there in Via Uruguay and searches would resume in September, after mid-September. But he said he'd found something out, something he couldn't be sure about, or swear to. There was a woman who could be Massimina Meleschi working for a government official in Via Uruguay, or thereabouts. He said the family of this official had gone to the coast, probably with this woman, to San Benedetto del Tronto.

There was no point therefore, I thought, returning to San Savino and to the festa of Sant'Albertino, though I'd like to have seen the white friars again. I'd also like to have gone back to Doglio, maybe one evening, and gone to see what there really was behind those bramble bushes, how wide those holes were, to look at the soil, to work out why it was so red and so yellow, to go to the mine to see if they had a job for me.

But for the very reason that I'd like to have done all these things and most of all to have gone back to my house, to San Savino, to open my front door, to walk in, to find everything there and then go out to the hill at the back and also go bathing in the river . . . for the very reason that I'd like to have done all these things, I stayed at Rome thinking about them and saw my house before me. And on its door, secured with chains, I kept imagining there was a woman there who seemed to be playing a mandolin— a mandolin or a guitar—like no woman had ever played at San Savino, at least not that I had seen.

Through August I wandered Rome, crossed the bridges, strolled its streets and piazzas. I drank lemonades and ate ice creams and went into the coolness of the churches.

I had stopped studying for a while and was taking it easy. I was quite sure to find Massimina in September, so I had no need to worry and could be certain about what I'd do with Massimina in September. I had money, besides the 100,000 lire, and thought both of us could go back to San Savino, where I could find work as a machine operator. Or, if she preferred, we could sell everything and go to live on the coast, in Pesaro or Senigallia. I ate ice creams and thought of Massimina and looked at church facades and took long walks around the city, past old palaces, under the shadow of their cornices. Each place seemed like the corner of that building in the painted backdrop I had seen in the Contessa Carsidoni's garden. The only place where I felt in touch, in company, was under the trees along the riverbank. I felt a new energy and a certainty that I was coming to the end of one chapter of my life and beginning another, that this would bring less strife and be more positive and that, as time passed, my studies would become clearer, yielding definite results, one after the other, like successive feast days, as the moon slowly waxes.

In September I went back to the police officer, who still knew nothing.

Around the end of September, he said the picture was vague. He had no news but told me to be careful, not to do anything rash, since the official was a counsellor of state, in a position of power. I could see a sheet of paper in front of him with a telephone number at the bottom. I read it, then said goodbye. All I wanted, I said, was to exercise my rights—first to know where my wife was, then to see her.

'You're sure your wife wants to see you?' the policeman asked. I looked at him, paused for a moment, then said yes. The policemen kept his silence, then folded the paper.

'Very well,' he said.

Once outside I looked for a bar to telephone the number I had seen on the sheet of paper. The phone at the other end made a loud noise. I imagined it ringing in a large hall. The consigliere came from one corner of this hall and picked up the receiver.

'Hello,' he said.

'Hello,' I replied.

'Hello.'

'Hello,' I said, 'my name is Lupinelli, I'd like to speak to Massimina.'

'Who is it?' the consigliere asked.

'Lupinelli,' I replied.

'Who are you, what do you want?'

'I want to talk to Massimina.'

'Massimina isn't here.'

'But Massimina lives there?' I asked.

'Massimina isn't here, you're not to call.'

'But I'm one of the family,' I said.

'Which one?' the consigliere asked. Fortunately, he was angry at having to answer the phone and remained there to work off his anger.

'I'm close family,' I said.

'Oh yes?!' the consigliere said.

'Yes,' I said.

'From where?' asked the consigliere.

'I'm from the Marche,' I replied.

'Where?'

'From Doglio.'

'Never heard of it.'

'I said Doglio because it's the largest place, but I'm from Riempimento di Serra, like Massimina.'

'Massimina isn't here,' the consigliere said.

I was now sure that Massimina lived there and could happily say: 'I'll call back when she returns.'

'No, you're not to telephone,' the Consigliere said. 'This telephone is not for you. If you're family then you know how to make yourself known, how to write, where you can meet Massimina.'

'But I'm passing through,' I said, 'I have to be back in the Marche this evening and want to discuss certain business with Massimina.'

'They have business in the Marche too?' asked the consigliere. 'You can go back to the Marche. Return there and stay there. You can write to Massimina if you wish, though she has no kind of business. Don't go bothering this girl, she wants to work. You keep to your farming. Work the land, put your faith in the land, don't go telephoning.'

With these words the consigliere put down the telephone. I felt no excitement and was almost disappointed to find Massimina like this. Perhaps I was disappointed to find her there in Rome, in Via Uruguay, which I had seen. I imagined her by one of those windows with the curtains drawn. But she was there, and I had to get her away. I had always thought I'd find her among a retinue of Marchigiani, with a family connected to some other town, at Prima Porta or somewhere else. And since all those peasants would have protected her, and it would have been harder to drag her away from that retinue than from Doglio, I imagined putting up a fight and then winning. In Via Uruguay, I thought, it would be enough to ring the doorbell at the main entrance and wait for her to come down by the lift, looking pallid with her suitcase. But this pallor of hers suddenly made me love her all the more, and I felt an urge to go to Via Uruguay, to the foot of one of those black-and-white marble stairways that I had seen, and to take her away.

When I tried to call again, the telephone rang even louder. The consigliere jumped out from the corner, more quickly this time, as though he'd been waiting for the phone to ring.

'Hello,' he said.

'Hello,' I said. 'It's Lupinelli, I'd like to talk to Massimina.'

'Oh!' he said. 'Lupinelli or Ceciarelli, you're lying, I warn you, I'll have you arrested before you have time to put down the receiver. You're a cheat, don't telephone again, and what is more, Massimina is not here, she doesn't live here and, as far as you're concerned, she'll never live here!'

'And who are you to talk like this?' I asked.

'This is my house and, I'll tell you if you wish to know. I'm Avvocato Consigliere Luigi Frugiferenti.'

'Thank you, Avvocato Consigliere Frugiferenti,' I said. 'Then please ask Massimina to come to the telephone and speak to me.'

'Massimina doesn't wish to speak to a bully like you, and even if she were weak enough to do so, I would stop her.'

'Oh!' I said, 'I know perfectly well from your title that you're a bully yourself, quite accustomed to using the tyranny of power. I know perfectly well that you think you can decide what your servants should feel. But remember, Signor Avvocato Consigliere, that I am no servant and I'm not afraid of your power, or of you as a person. You are committing a further abuse by not letting Massimina speak to me, but remember, you'll get no thanks for this further gesture of authority.'

The consigliere was so angered by this exchange that he carried on talking, but I left the bar and went wandering around Rome. I thought Rome was beginning to seem broader and less indifferent. I thought I had found the way to fight against this city which, until then, had refused to notice me, to show me any of its faces, to accept and respond to my grasp. Every part of Via Uruguay seemed to be conspiring with Avvocato Frugiferenti, extending into the different yellow-and-white buildings in which the tyranny that subjugated the whole of poor Italy was concentrated, the tyranny that rejected science and raised and nurtured the toil of people like poor Massimina.

The battle to be fought against Avvocato Frugiferenti also renewed my eagerness to study, and I felt more clearly what I should do, to release Massimina and take her back to San Savino, away from the corruption of Rome and the university, to return to the lucidity of San Savino, which I considered the most ordered and welcoming of workplaces.

Back in my lodgings, I looked at the statuette. Its face confirmed these resolutions and this eagerness and lucidity. The statuette had never yielded to Rome, barely altering, never conceding to the sudden changes of light, as if this were the light of San Savino or any other place. Like the statuette, I had to follow my own path and had to pursue my plans, never yielding to Rome's obstacles or other difficulties created for me by the world around. I had to remember, as I could see from the statuette's face, not to submit to persecution nor to give up my plans in my fight against power and society. I had to go on regardless, in the belief that with my resolutions I was pursuing the very path that would benefit and improve authority and society and would therefore destroy their reasons for fighting against me.

Avvocato Frugiferenti was an arrogant little man from whom I needed to break free, not by defeating him and destroying his arrogance, a product of his stupidity and his absolute devotion to power, but by denying such power and its hierarchies and its constraints, by reducing Frugiferenti in this way to nothing more than a poor envious hound, to nothing more than a broom that stands up if it is propped against the wall.

I telephoned again that afternoon, hoping the Avvocato might be asleep, but he was ready once again to leap at the telephone and hurl insults.

'Remember that your authority is nil,' I said. 'No newspaper, not *Il Tempo* nor *Il Messaggero*, will convince me that you're an authority. There's no city council, no police office, no nameplate in Via Uruguay that can put you before me in any courtroom. Poor ignorant folk like you, servants of a state that exists only in your titles and your chapters, are vanquished by science and have already been abandoned by history. You're a poor monarchist with no other protection. You're the one who should be seeking my advice, who should be looking to me and recognizing that I'm the one with the strength to move forward, dragging you and your government job behind me.'

The consigliere at the other end was still talking about police, law courts and prison and had no other arguments, apart from those poor utterances of the kind used by lunatics, loners, oddballs. I asked him then what logical connection he could see between the power of the atomic bomb and the power of his authority, and moreover what connection he could see between his authority and the use of atomic energy for peaceful aims; or what philosophical nexus, however flimsy, did he manage to put up around the windows of his house in Via Uruguay, between his discretion, his arrogance and the democratic nature of parliamentary power, which formed the basis of his office and therefore of his responsibility. He shouted 'subversive lunatic' and called me a 'poor fool', and I replied that his days were now numbered, not because he would soon become paralysed, like all arrogant men, but because soon, one day when he has the courage to reflect on it, maybe while relieving himself, he would feel the bladder of his authority and his arrogance suddenly deflate, turn inside out, he would discover that he was a poor consigliere with no counsel to give, nor to receive, so that he would tell Massimina not to open the windows to prevent the draught from catching his skin and carrying him away.

The consigliere ended by saying he would call the police and hoped I would have the effrontery to turn up at his house, so that he would have the pleasure of watching my arrest and of taking hold of me to put on the handcuffs. I asked him whether he had never realized, with that authority of his, that he had spent his whole life doing nothing other than handcuffing people, and that if he hadn't realized it, then he had lost the only true pleasure that his authority might have given him; that to be a true consigliere of a truly absolute yet falsely democratic and bourgeois state, he would have to consciously enjoy this opportunity to catch and imprison others through whatever indictment, each indictment signed moreover by himself, and in this way he would also have gained more pleasure from his conversations with his colleagues and the obsequiousness of his minions, their smiles, and their fear, and gained more pleasure from keeping slaves and corrupting their intelligence—assuming that a consigliere's minion, or anyone aspiring to any career, could think of using or showing intelligence, assuming then that intelligence could ever appear among such hierarchies and grades and not be obliterated by the first signature and by the first rubber stamp. I told him that I needed no court of law to pass judgement on him, but needed my science alone, and my conscience, and that I absolved him in the same way that wretched, worthless, incapable outcasts are absolved, and that his authority was no more than the preening and the empty shriek of a cockerel. And instead of calling out for no purpose, at the risk of splitting the veins of his neck, and instead of scratching about pointlessly in the ground with his tail feathers, I could give him a few pieces of useful advice and teach him what to read and how to behave; and was therefore waiting, at that moment, for him to invite me to his house and to see Massimina again and also to give him this advice, in the sitting room, in front of a glass of marsala.

I spent the rest of the day wandering the streets of Rome, until late afternoon, when I went to buy a new suit, for I was sure I'd have to go and meet Massimina next day, or a day or two later.

I telephoned early next morning, when the consigliere would still have been asleep while Massimina would have been doing her servant's chores. It was indeed Massimina who answered, and I recognized her voice with its sighs, its faltering sighs between one syllable and the next.

'You're still pestering me, you're still pestering me,' she said, 'and now you insult His Excellency—you're really mad, you really are mad!'

I said I was disappointed by such words, for I wanted only to talk about love, to tell her I missed her company and how I wanted to be with her, how much I thought about her and how I saw her face and her moles—even at that moment—and how I could feel the telephone touching her lips and her moles, and ruffling the curls of her hair; and how I imagined her holding her hands by her mouth, and her knees together, and how I hoped she felt some emotion, even just a pang of sorrow, after being apart for so long, and how I hoped she would realize, regardless of all other questions, that she still had some affection towards me and, more than that, some feeling of love.

But she said, 'Go away, go away, I never want to see you again, you're the ruin of my life, it would have been better if I'd never met you. I should have listened to what people said, listened to the priests as well, to those people you mocked, those you deliberately mocked. I should have listened to what the cards had told me, never to marry a good-for-nothing like you. And you took advantage of my poor heart, and my innocence, and you seemed what you were not, and used your wickedness against a poor defenceless girl, and hurt me not only with your hands but also with your insults and your rebellions. And there's no way of going back, for you are damned, marked out by God, and I am now ruined forever, and can no longer be blessed with love or with a family, so don't make me lose this last hope, the last hope left, of serving His Excellency and living in peace.'

'You're talking against yourself,' I said, 'just as you've been taught by the priests and their servants, those who control you even inside your own home. You have no control even over your own conscience, just as you have no control over your own body, if you won't allow it any stirring of emotion towards me. He is no Excellency, there's no point boasting about being his servant, imagining it's some great position. A dog in Via Uruguay is given more affection and is better treated than you. If you lose your con- science, then you're losing the only good thing you have, which is what you could have from me, along with the encouragement of my rebellion, on the day of your liberation. Get ready to meet me soon, sooner than you think. And don't drop to the ground when you meet me and don't faint, for I need you so that I can smile, and put my trust in you, and take you by the hand and walk off together.'

Massimina moaned and groaned and begged me and cried about her unhappiness. At the end she said: 'Leave me, now—if His Excellency finds me with you at the telephone, he'll have my brothers called, and send the police to arrest you.'

'All right, I'll let you go,' I said, 'and I'll give you a hug and I'll tell you again, no army of policemen nor maybe even chains can keep me from you. I'm stronger than them all, and you know it, and with this strength I'll look after you, and me, and our happiness.'

I dressed straightaway in my new suit and went to Via Uruguay, thinking that Massimina would soon be leaving for the market and that I could surprise her, still trembling after the telephone call, and could take her away as I had promised. I asked for directions to a market near Via Uruguay and stood at the entrance. After a moment, as I moved away to light a cigarette, I saw Massimina by some bank offices with a policeman in uniform. I hurried towards her with my arms open, to give her a hug in front of the people in the market and in front of the policeman who, on seeing us embrace, could hardly have stopped us, and would be held back by the power of our love. But when Massimina saw me, she looked down at her shopping bag and started to scream and shriek in such a piercing voice that I stopped. The policeman stepped in and approached me but then, following his orders, turned to Massimina to protect her and escorted her through the crowd to the place where she lived on Via Uruguay.

After that, each time I passed Via Uruguay I saw the policeman at the doorway, and over the next few days I saw policemen with Massimina each time she went out.

I kept watch for ten days, then wrote a letter to Consigliere Frugiferenti asking for a truce and asking him to let Massimina go outside just once, as a test, to see whether she would refuse my proposals, which were the honest and affectionate proposals of her husband and which came from every true sentiment, from my heart and my mind. I wrote that our conflicts were the result of our different conceptions of life and state, of our different philosophies, which were both noble as such, even if mine was supported by a wealth of up-to-date scientific learning, whereas his might be supported by Latin and by a historical knowledge that was now old-fashioned; that in any event, the two of us ought to reach a truce on equal terms, recognizing, on my part, deference and respect only for his age rather than for his rank or authority; that he should therefore send Massimina out alone, once, in the daytime, if he feared that the night, of which he was certainly afraid, in the same way that the whole of his philosophy and the whole of his history had always been afraid of the night, of obscurity and of divinity . . . if he feared that the night might scare Massimina or at least unsettle her and make her more easily persuaded by my proposals and my insistence. In the daytime I would appear as I was and my words would be as clear as the lines on my face, and if Massimina chose to follow me, this would be none other than a sign of condemnation for what had arisen against us and against our love.

But over the following days, Massimina was always in the company of a policeman. I tried telephoning early in the morning, but if it was Massimina who answered, she hung up immediately or stood there sobbing, not uttering a word, or saying yes and no incoherently, still crying in despair, as if with that telephone call I were somehow attacking her feelings.

One morning the telephone was engaged, and it was engaged throughout the day and for several days. There was no answer any longer. I spent several days after that in Via Uruguay, waiting under a small tree which greeted me each day by dropping its leaves onto me. The police would watch me from the other side of the street but made no attempt to speak. It was they who were in the wrong. They had no right to assist in the injustice that Signor Consigliere Frugiferenti was committing against me, and against Massimina herself.

So one day I went to the police station in Via Uruguay to tell them I had found my wife but couldn't go near her because of the wrongful interference of the police, who were parties to a personal abuse of power, unless it was also a public abuse of power, namely, that of Signor Frugiferenti, who was preventing me from seeing and speaking to my wife. The policeman said nothing but took me to a plainclothes officer. This officer told me he couldn't accept my accusation of police interference or abuse of power by His Excellency Consigliere Frugiferenti, and he was doing this for my own benefit, for if he chose to accept such an accusation, he'd have to arrest me immediately. He said he could consider my case from the moment in which I had begun it with a complaint against my wife for deserting the matrimonial home. But against this report, he said, my wife had made another complaint against me for persistent and aggravated cruelty, for failure to give financial support, for embezzlement, and for making persistent threats against her and other members of her family. I began to laugh and said that Frugiferenti had more than a finger in this pie, and even a child could make this pie with better pastry.

'Very well,' said the officer, 'I'm not here to judge, but there are other formalities I now have to complete. Tell me where you're living in Rome, how long you've been here, your registered address, your occupation.'

156

I said I was living at Porta Portese and was here to study. He smiled and asked if I was a student. I said yes, adding that I was something more than a student. He asked if I was enrolled at one of the university faculties, or was an assistant, or a university professor. I said I was a freelance scholar. He told me he'd have to expel me from Rome and would issue an immediate expulsion order against me for being of no fixed abode, vagrancy, harassment, et cetera. He called two policemen and repeated what he had just said. They typed out the order and dragged me away. I was forcibly dragged down the steps with a number of beatings, after which they regained their hypocritical composure outside the front door and took me to the railway station, with further heavy abuse. I couldn't even get a coffee and had to wait four hours for a local train to Ancona. The policemen asked every now and then whether I had calmed down, poking fun at me with questions about my studies. But I replied that every single hair on their southern Italian heads, including those under their helmets, had been counted, just as mine on my bare unrepentant head had been counted too. I told them it was fortunate that my studies made them laugh and, in all honesty, I hoped the whole of humanity would one day laugh even more, out of sheer joy.

I had been banished from Rome and had to leave by that train. But all was not lost, and I thought of poor Frugiferenti who was waiting in the shadows of his hall for the telephone to ring, ready to stand up with all his poor excellency of belly and trousers, and his filthy mouth, waiting for someone to talk to, waiting to further his vocation of insulting whoever dared to stand up to him, whoever was still free, who had not yielded to his bullying. Then I realized that inside that train I was free, even though I'd been banished and branded, and I started looking at the sun which was not so high, for the whole sky was streaked with many white clouds and many burning lenses: the sun was in the stones that filled the fields of those farms, sown one after another like bones that had resurfaced after a battle. And yet the sun was on some invisible stalk, which I couldn't see from the train but whose reflection and subtle vibration I saw. That Roman countryside, which is different from the Marche, has no hills and ditches and waves of sentiment, but has this great, extended and lacerated brow: and at that moment it had this brow which sought to rise up before me with all the reflections and the rays of its light which jostled and collided like the material of so many thoughts. I began also to see grass in an occasional hollow, which remained narrow so as not to lose its shade and its vigour, or lay in the shadow of some gully for a moment of respite and to gather the substance of one of those thoughts that smouldered in the air and reached as far as to touch the train, to bounce over its wheels and even to enter through the windows, as far as my feet.

The train was filled with all these shards of light, and I was touched and stirred by them. I was going home. This had been my intention, for I remembered this was what I had planned, to leave Rome at some point, whether I had found Massimina or not, to avoid sinking to my knees like those poor lupini sellers with their gleaming chests and their even greater wonderment. I would return to Rome once my treatise was complete, when my science could accompany me and could safely present itself in my guise, so that I would be spared from all the battles against ignorance and authority.

I gazed at the sky and the trees and now at the countryside towards the Sabine Hills, where the slopes and expanses of olive trees began, interrupting the first brow and hiding the stones; and then, in November, the sun quickly vanishes at dusk. I looked at those realms around me and began to think, after refocusing the basis of my thought on that land, on its Sabine gorges and on the sky's absorbent atmosphere, that every entity which understands laws, which understands how those laws that stretched between me, my train and that mouth of sky and countryside were certain and scientifically true, and which, beyond these laws, understands plant and animal realms and ourselves, is the invention and the making of a generation of individuals that existed before, whose life ended after they had achieved these things, or whose existence continues so long as it operates the mechanics of those laws that keeps this immense mouth open.

Having refocused the basis of my thought on those surroundings, I could proceed to consider how *plants and animals, in reality, serve particular needs and were therefore created with a highly developed system in such a way that each species is nurtured and reconstructed with the method established and devised for it, so that it can adopt the behaviour required to perform the specific task. Since plants and souls each help and assist the other and adopt distinct forms of behaviour using better and better methods, and since such methods though different tend to complement each other, they explain how they were designed gradually, and therefore how the brain motor of their constructors has followed a certain order of development and has not suddenly disgorged, through a merely physical capability, a series of things one after another, made once and for all and no longer to be considered. Given that plants and animals are not the same in all regions of the earth and yet we humans are alike, this shows that the kind of producer-generation that made us was divided into various levels of individual inventors and that, at least at the beginning, every kind of individual would design and build according to their skills and according to their possibilities and that both of these were influenced by environment, level of development and the presence, among these too, of certain eminent figures and certain priests.*

Continuing on with these thoughts I managed to fix in my mind, clearly, and with a clarity and consistency as obvious as that of the seat on which I was sitting, that by seeking to calculate *the relationships between the future of the artificial and the past of the natural, we find proof that the generations of individuals that follow one another eternally in the universe tend to invent and to create other generations, before their own generations die out. If, on the one hand, the brain motor improves its scientific skills, on the other, it moves further towards the end of its capability to develop science. It is then necessary to deal with progressive civilizations by creating another brain motor, in other words, another generation comprising other individuals with improved skills, with motorial senses more developed than our own, and therefore those of automaton-creators.*

All of this is the most exact explanation and most perfect demonstration of evolutionary progress. Knowledge about our solar system, as I told His Excellency Consigliere Frugerenti, who laughed about the Sputnik, will provide us with scientific results that fully adhere to the propositions in my treatise, whose position and significance today remain unclear, and which will provide proof and give practical force to these results so that it will be possible to move at last towards the progressive civilization of automaton-creators and towards the harmonious coexistence of mankind in universal eternity.

For example, during the night on the train, I thought: how and where did the various generations before us live? How and where will the various individuals who come after us live? *Was the Earth transformed for us, before we were created as individuals? Shall we transform other planets for the generation we will create?* I have managed to keep these questions and note them down in my treatise, to write them down clearly at the end of a chapter in which I had set out the considerations leading up to them, namely, those thoughts that had come to mind as I gazed at the Roman countryside through the stabbing of all those shards of messages and light that were exploding in and around the train, and around me, on my expulsion from Rome.

There was no bus for Pergola that evening when I reached Fabriano. I sat in the station bar with my expulsion order laid out in front of me so that no one could disturb me, no one could throw me out, not least because the police kept coming and going with hands on guns and with military helmets. I spent the night at that metal table in the bar, happy enough with the tarnished light that came from the liqueur bottles, with that company of policemen and railway workers, happy enough with a few sweets—mints, liquorice, or cinnamon pastilles—to stop my mouth turning dry with sleep and to keep back the smell of my breath. Meanwhile I felt the night thicken and creak around the station and the blue panes of the buffet. Every so often it was shattered by a train, but night descended once again from the surrounding hills and came with its great cold feet, heavy with November mud, up to the door of the bar. The night was warning me, tapping at the windows. It was searching for me, as if it wanted me on its stage, impatient to have me back in the Marche. I could feel it preparing the landscape, roads, farmland for me, that it had kept some fruit for me, high on the branches of some sister tree.

In the morning I drank my coffee with eyes closed, so as not to see dawn inside the bar, then went towards the bus stop. When the bus left, there were already many sparrows in the streets—the tops of the trees and their forks were already luminous, and they drooled a froth that would keep them alive for another day. I looked up and saw the pale sun, for the bus was now out of Fabriano, and around me I could see those stone walls that go as far as Doglio. At the top of each poor field, forlorn above the stones, was an almond tree that welcomed me to the Marche countryside. Beyond the gorges were the red soils of Serra Sant'Abbondio and, lower down, the valleys and steep slopes of the Cesano and, after these, here at last, my home territory, the great river bend, the pinnacle of Frontone and the plain of Acquaviva as far as Nerone. And here, the hamlet of Monlione, all oaks and light-blue clay. The pinnacle of Frontone was pink and shimmered. At the far end of this whole great valley, it seemed as if someone was striking an anvil with a hammer, in the distance, where celestial blades of frost broke spreading the sound.

'O Marche, sweet Marche, O sweet land of the Marche, sweet mark of madness, O sweet morning to be on the summit of the Marche, to be free and to know which road to take home, to know the fields and the fruit trees that turn bare in November and fall to sleep; to recognize the weights and the measures, the girth of each peach and apple tree, the colours of the vetch, of the broom, of the bracken in the ditches, the sound of rough gravel on the lanes, the thud of bridges, the spouting of water.'

With a stone I felt I could have struck anything, just as a lover might have struck his beloved tenderly on the breast or thigh. There was even snow on the peak of Catria, and those white streaks in the sky that mark the city of Urbino far away. I could hear the farmers in every valley, but as I began to think of them, I was caught by Massimina's absence: 'O Marche,' I said, 'O land of the Marche, I know how thankless your folly can be, how fickle your nature can be. Shall I now start praising your perverse beauty, the cruel fixity of your nature? I am still the same Anteo, and I'm back to pursue my thoughts, not to be tempted by your fruits. I have other fruits to construct, I have people to free, and their countryside too—from death, from days spent staring blankly at the countryside and at nature, awaiting death, doing nothing that might become better than death itself.'

I returned to reality. I arrived home and found all the doors had been broken down. Even the chains I had tied to them had been smashed and left in pieces in front of the house. Nothing had been touched inside. Everything was in the same place, though the doors of the chest had been kicked in. But this intrusion must have happened long ago, soon after my departure, and my house had obviously fought back and overcome that band of marauders, those I had seen several times getting pleasure from kicking the bloated stomachs of cows or horses that had collapsed with foot-and-mouth or colic, content and convinced they weren't yet dead themselves and could vent their fury on those whose weakness and fault it was to die one day sooner. My house had fought back, perhaps by frightening them or perhaps by overcoming them with its mysterious matter, until it made them indifferent and then its slaves, like the whole of nature and the whole countryside. Those marauders must have kept away from the house for some time because the winter pears were still on the trees, and the pots were still full of lavender and basil. Even the animals I had set free hadn't been slaughtered, for I could see several rabbits scampering away and heard the clucking of hens: this clucking gave me the idea that the roof of the house was in good order, that its tiles echoed, and I could feel safe. Inside, I went through each room one by one, tapped the walls, could feel that the floors were solid, and went to my room at the top to look for the opening pages of my treatise behind the bricks that I dislodged. On the floor below, even Massimina's belongings and our bed were still there. The marauders had only damaged the doors and a few cupboards. As always, they had beaten on the bloated drum of death, their own death.

Over the next few days, after I had noted down in the treatise those thoughts I had considered and settled during the journey, and after I had delivered half of the expulsion order to the brigadier of the carabinieri at Frontone, I set about mending the doors of my house, for winter would soon arrive. I tried to round up the rabbits and hens that had gone wild, repaired the stakes in the chicken fence, and discovered where the hens had been laying their eggs so that I could put them back inside the pens. I then took a walk around my fields and saw that grapes and clover had been pillaged, especially around the edges, but some grapes were still hanging from the vines further in, withered and full of blight. I gathered as much fruit as I could and stored it carefully in the rooms of the house, since the sheds would let in rain. While I was storing my crop of grapes, pears, walnuts, and maize, I wrote in my treatise:

Free will is the compass of knowledge; the environment is the mirror of the imagination. Free will continually improves with exercise and its services are always more exact, whereas the environment likewise develops constantly, but according to the needs of progressive civilizations, and in satisfaction of these needs.

My surroundings felt strange, yet I was drawn by a nostalgia I had never known before.

Each day passed and re-emerged, and I spent each one moving from place to place: the day and I had the same tasks and the same problems. I felt attuned to all that went on around me, whether it was a tree that bent in the wind or the grim figure of a cloud that moved across the hills. I felt indeed a visceral connection with the Earth and with its sounds and felt that my hunger came and was satisfied by certain colours of the countryside and certain animal calls. I had become more attentive and skilled than the animals—more skilled than the rabbits with their broods in the woods, than the hens that had settled down by the stream. When I went hunting, I could almost always surprise them, and often with such skill that I'd suddenly see their dark dilated eyes half a pace in front. As they trembled, I would keep so calm that I could see the surrounding objects reflected in the pupil of their eye: a tuft of grass, a tree trunk, my own figure magnified, and I could see how beneath these objects the liquid of their eye froze for an instant and how, at almost the same moment, its reflexes triggered the brain in its skull, not far from the eye, beneath its furry or feathered face, telling it to escape. I could feel the click of the nerve centres and the mechanisms of the head, the crack of the membrane in the rabbit's ears and the pecking of the hen's beak. I could see the animal overcome its fear, shake its body, launch itself, and very often the soil from its sudden escape would fly up at me. But I was ruthless and would strike the animals with a club, breaking them in half; or I'd catch them in a sack, since I kept my gun in reserve and saved the shots for hares, foxes, and geese that would pass on the first moon of the new year. Nor did I want the neighbours to hear me shooting too much and thought those cartridges might be more useful for a certain project that began to form within me, inspired by many confused ideas about that life and which I also found encouraged by the numerous indulgences of that same life.

At home I ate standing, pacing around the table, and looking out of the window. As I was chewing, I would gaze at the trees, the sparrows, the mud, and every scrap of meat I ate became a part of that life and gave me a pleasure that moved me and brought me in touch with all things, so much as to make me feel like a sword that could stab and strike down everything. I often ate olives, roots, raw garlic, and would then turn tearful and bitter before the glass in the window, or a tree beneath the wind, or a field.

After a while, around mid-December, it began to snow. Then, before the snow shook and shrivelled everything in the fields, while a wind gusted around me and swirled across my eyes and my hands, I went into the fields to gather turnips, beet, and the roots that I had at first ignored since hunting had been so easy, and because of the great amount of fruit I seemed to have gathered in to store. I hadn't even collected much wood and realized I would need more to get through winter. Then, as the sleet wind blew, I went into the woods to gather bundles of sticks and to pull out a few logs. As I was working with a billhook, I cut a large gash in my left leg—a deep violet wound that bled little and lay open around the bone, like a slit in the trunk of a poplar. I sat straight down on the ground and, little by little, to distract my thoughts, started considering the woods, how they lay beneath the snow—how the snow settled on their whole structure, the trees, junipers, moss, the membranes of the ferns—and I saw how the life of this vegetation came away from the edge laden with snow and thickened like dark blood in the more sheltered points closer to the ground. The woods left an inert, lifeless mantle for the snow, and every so often, in some place, this mantle fell, and I heard the thud as it dropped. Meanwhile it continued to snow, and the snow bathed my shinbone and my wound and the sock which I had had to roll down to my shoe. I heard a blackbird flutter away leaving a dusting of snow behind its black tail. Down below, towards the stream, I also heard a larger bird scavenging between the water and the bank. I gathered my wood and returned home, where I bandaged the wound. I sat by the window and the pain that grew in my leg was not dissimilar to this life of mine. But it was another way of keeping in touch with the whole countryside and with the calendar, and to me it seemed that through the pain and the swelling of the leg, which corresponded to some part of the countryside, I was close to being overwhelmed by that life and by that cycle of time that was San Savino, winter, snow, and countryside, and my vain solitude. I was wholly isolated by the winter, and my feelings, like the woods, had surrendered much of themselves, gathering their strength in a more sheltered inner nest which I had yet to discover. My studies, indeed, were not going well. More than anything, I wanted to go off hunting, to go setting traps along the lanes, even beyond my own land, in the hope of catching a plump goose or a turkey, perhaps even one of my neighbours' pigs.

I built and set traps, then lay in wait under a tree or in a hide, or at home. I was always anxious, imagining the trap going off at any moment and the agony of the captured animal. The first animal I caught was a beech marten. It was still alive, and I left it alive in an empty rabbit hutch in front of the house. I limped off—the mouth of the violet wound still gaped open—into the snow, with my traps, and my gun over my shoulder. One day I met a fox. It stopped to look at me, maybe pretending to be a dog, since it had no chance of escape. As I raised my hand slowly towards the butt of the gun to take it from my shoulder, it twitched its whiskers and gently turned its tail as if to gather strength and choose a direction. When it saw my gun, now pointing at its stomach, it made no effort to escape. It just snarled and threw itself towards the shot, to die immediately. It died with its teeth bared and a bitter sneer that made my cruelty seem shameful. I took this poor fox by its legs and threw it in my neighbour's yard.

Hunting, which I liked so much, was another way of giving my whole heart to that winter and to that condition of mine, though I often tried to deceive myself, with my leg wounded and bare in front of the fire, into thinking that hunting and watching animals escape and die was a way of testing out my studies and seeing how the machines of those elementary beings reacted. In fact, I was moving towards a state of savagery, even if, fortunately, I was moving alone and without the help and justification of a whole group and a whole society.

I was consoled by the idea of always being alone and always being a rebel. Indeed, I decided not even to go to the store to buy salt, matches, or other things I might need, and resolved to invent some way of managing without the need for any supplies. Hunting, in the meantime, kept me busier than ever, since there was a great migration of thrushes, blackbirds, and even ducks over the streams and the valleys of the Cinisco. I had only a few shots left and didn't want to use them on thrushes, blackbirds, or even ducks unless I had to, so put out rough nets over clumps of ivy and the tops of junipers, then took cover, ready to pull the rope when I saw two or three thrushes perch on the berries or fly into the junipers. For the ducks, I had invented a kind of bait, made with pins and maize kernels which I floated in the stream on leaves fixed to a twig and stuck into the mud on the bank. But only a few took the bait and if one of them was caught, the others flew off in their V-shaped formations high in the sky.

These duck formations were another sign of the approaching winter, until I reached January, the day of my birthday. That day, I heard voices down my chimney and saw a group of neighbours pass on the road. They had been to dig out badgers and to sing 'La Pasquella' at some of the houses in Monlione and Fenigli. When they reached my house, I was at the window and they started shouting, but in good cheer, shouting greetings, and one of them left a flask of wine for me, pressed into the snow. I was touched by this and could now take part in the celebrations up to Epiphany and after my birthday. A flock of thrushes gathered on the rosemary bush in my vegetable patch and flitted about, pecking at each other, as close-packed as if they were in the corner of a handkerchief. I took the gun and fired a shot from the window which left nine thrushes flat on the ground beneath the rosemary. One was injured and flapped about in front of me. I limped across and tried to catch it. It flew and hopped and could still hop when I took it by the tail, hopping into the hutch where the beech marten was. I picked up the thrushes, took them up to the kitchen, and put them on the table. I looked at the figure of that line of thrushes, then at all the signs on the wall, and concluded that I was as good as dead. Even from the window, I could find no other interpretation.

The day wandered on, now sunk to the groin, now caught by the dark immersion of the night. Its footsteps were immense, and it shook off drizzle and mud that ended in hoar frost. I tried then to respond and realized I first had to destroy the traps. Straightaway I had to side with those animals, those thrushes and hares I'd been hunting until then. If I had to eat, if I had to find food, then I had to do it by battling against my neighbours' lands, snatching from them rather than snatching from myself by killing those thrushes that came to visit. From these decisions I went straight back to thinking about science. I began by realizing I was going back in time, back in history, to my human state of lone hunter and lover of nature, going back just like the man with no education and no understanding of science.

Nature is always the same, and thrushes, hares, ducks, and badgers always behave in the same way, and the days always go back and forth, through weeks and months and seasons of summer heat and hoar frost, always leaving marks that are always the same, always raising water and mud or shaking trees or striking at the woods or forming crags or hurling stones down from the mountains or making another rock pool in the rivers or swelling the currents between the clay cliffs. But man must not proceed like this, because his knowledge—which is the best part of him and his most natural expression—doesn't go in this way and never goes backwards: he has never rejected any of his own propositions, to which he has always given consideration and has then always absorbed and carried further. Knowledge always has the awareness to seek and eagerly confirm a truth that is always larger and never contradicts itself, which remains whole, which loses no part of itself and relinquishes none of its outer surfaces; which moves forward and carries everything with it, just as the mind does, more so than human life. The mind, which can never stop and always tends to build (unless someone buries it, like those I have encountered in my life, like those who wrote on the walls of my house have done), tends to turn itself into something greater, richer.

During those days at the end of January in which the wind froze everything to fix a whole month of ice, I decided to apply myself once more to my studies and spend as little time as I could hunting, or looking after the storehouses, or contemplating nature. I thought how that blackened stone ledge of my fireplace had already seen everything and had grilled whole generations of animals and felt the blast of cold north winds and smelt the smoke of logs and bundles of twigs for at least a hundred years. I now organized myself better and tended my wound without further delay. I treated it, disinfected it with salt and water, and tied it with bandages. I set the beech marten free and went to the store to buy everything I needed, including ten cartridges for the thieving I had to do in order to limit the time I wasted and to intensify my studies. The next day I went down to the stream, followed it almost to the bridge and climbed behind the line of oaks to my neighbour's yard. I bashed the pig over the head with the butt of my gun, hauled it onto my shoulders, and returned home. I butchered the meat in the way I had been taught by the pig killer and carefully hid all its parts in the wardrobe, behind Massimina's bedsheets. Then I passed in front of my neighbour's house so I could be seen on my way to the shop. I bought some newspapers and ordered a book I wanted to read. I heard in the shop that Liborio was now the parish priest of Acquaviva.

The next day I went to Acquaviva to see him. As I walked, I saw a ray of sunlight that shone over and warmed the slopes of Frontone, those slopes alone, and a few fields going down towards Acquaviva. It was a single ray of sunlight that moved in front of me and came to lick my shoes and my shins—these alone, to the height of the roadside markers and gravel piles and the few remaining stalks that stood upright in the undergrowth pressed down by the snow. The sunlight didn't reach even as high as my knees, but it kept me company and drew me along with the same confidence as my good intentions, stretching now as far as Acquaviva, while behind the village swirled the muddy breezes of another day and another valley.

As I walked, even beneath the sun, I could feel firm ground between the patches of snow, and the day was still firm and deep into winter, not yet tainted by slush and by the effect of spring— natural events as visible to science as to the gaze of the falcon.

Liborio had always appeared before me on days of bright sunlight, when there was never a contrast between Earth and Sun, as if the Earth were taking light from itself, because the Sun is never in front, or behind, or high, or low, in opposition. Liborio had always appeared silhouetted by the sky or the woods of Montevecchio, never against the light or bathed in shadow, but always calmly illuminated. And his noble pallor always fell from his brow over the whole of his body and over things, especially those objects which he lightly handled.

I was depending on Liborio to help draw me from my slumber and from those ordinary physical pleasures that had taken hold of me, from those tastes that remained in the corners of my drooling mouth like on the lips of a hound. I knew I was also encouraged by friendship and the desire to see and talk again to someone who was fond of me. I then felt the sun rise up my legs and reach a hand to my scarf. I walked and lifted my feet and my knees so that I wouldn't look like a rustic, even to others. Every now and then I clapped my hands to scare off a redbreast or a magpie that flew from the trees and went to witter elsewhere, over the thorn woods.

I crossed the bridge over the Acquaviva torrent and was soon in Liborio's parish. My path now climbed, and to ease my impatience I studied every tree stump, every bare patch of ground freed from the snow by some small landslip or by the wind, as if I were looking for violets or primroses or a sturdy clump of broom to help pull me up the shortcuts.

When I saw the houses of Acquaviva, I felt nervous and afraid that the village people might catch me by surprise and scorn the weakness that had led me to go looking for a friend, that they might surprise me as if in some guilty scheme, as if I were coming down from the mountains where I had been banished. I went straight to the church and entered through the main door.

The church was just like the one at San Savino and there was no trace of Liborio's gentleness. I half expected to find him by the altar, standing with the palms of his hands towards me. I saw the poor Stations of the Cross and saw the wood-wormed tabernacle. They looked much like Massimina's wardrobe and the broken cupboard I had left behind at home, and this made me sadder. I wanted not to feel embarrassed, so I went forward, towards the door of the sacristy, and rang the bell that is rung when the priest enters. From there I saw the sacristy, all lime-washed with a few nails on the walls. Taking another step forward, on a side wall I saw some palm crosses made of olives on a nail, and on another the priest's biretta. The lime-washed walls were softer than plaster and the opening in the middle to the corridor was white and indistinct and seemed natural, like a crevice or the edge of a piece of fabric. Liborio emerged from it, tall as a priest, pale, with the palms of his hands against the hem of the opening. He stood wide-eyed, proud, with no expression of surprise or curiosity and responded with a movement of his mouth when I gave my name.

'Yes, I'm Anteo,' I said, 'and I've come to see you.'

'You've come from San Savino?' he asked.

'Yes.'

'I've heard much about you,' he said, 'so much that in the end I couldn't keep track. So many things I could hardly understand. Thank you for coming to see me. I hope there might be some reason for your visit, and this reason might be some request or some need that I might answer and might help you to resolve.'

'I have nothing to ask,' I said. 'I've come here to see a person, and a friend. My plans are clear, though recently I've been in some confusion. But I'm sure to achieve a great result for the good of everyone, not for my own benefit, because with this result I'm not concerned about demonstrating the soundness of my reasons to my poor companions and neighbours.'

'This is right,' Liborio said. 'I have often thought about your projects and kept an eye—so far as I could—on what you were doing. I have seen how your projects have never been forsaken, how they have always been an inspiration to your life, even when you go too far. But I have also seen that your projects haven't brought the good you speak about, and very often you have used them merely as an instrument for rebellion, and consequently your life has become that of a rebel.'

'I propose doctrines and reforms, I do not persecute, and I do not accuse anyone with my theories, and I even justify the wickedness of Mordi, of other masters and their servants, and I give them a reason for all this, so that they can understand and rid themselves of their wickedness and their wrongs. But if anyone replies that they want to keep this society, then they must also keep the wrongs of this society, and therefore all the wrongs that it does, or thinks. I have to battle against these wrongs which I see so clearly, if only to avoid being just as guilty.'

'But that's not the whole reality!' Liborio said.

'What reality?' I asked.

'The reality in which we live,' he replied, 'society, responsibilities, and before that, religion, respect for marriage, the family and then our duties—work, respect for ourselves and for others, peace of mind, charity.'

'This reality doesn't exist,' I said, 'and has never existed. It's just a fiction that's been forced on the weakest. There are only two words for reality—humanity and science—and these two words mustn't be cancelled out by some absurd notion, which is your construction of reality. Humanity must break out from this prison, this threshold of ignorance, and be free to tackle its problems, with a self-awareness that must be transformed into the possibility of going beyond ourselves and the things around us. Mankind will then be free and able to act in a way that today is not even contemplated by the words that it uses. It won't be just another repetition of the same actions described by those words but in a different way; it won't be a repetition of the same action carried out in the same way and for the same end, which can then be described using different words. Behind this society, the words themselves are fictions and their ideas have become hypocrisy. To be clear, I have to say that in front of this society, and in this society, even according to the notions you have described, people have no option, in my view, but to steal, to abuse their power, to exploit, fornicate, deceive, mislead, offend, kill. The true actions to be performed in this society are those, and they should be described in those terms.'

Liborio was neither amused nor offended, showing no particular sign of approval or disapproval. All he said was, 'That's a utopia!'

'Of course,' I said, 'and it's for that utopia that I ask your friendship, not just because you know me and I know you, not just because we have met and because you know all about my life, or because I see you as a priest and saw you as a young student. I want your friendship for my utopia, and I want you to help me believe in it.'

'I can be your friend, since I'm already your friend,' he said, 'and I'm your friend for many reasons. But if you want to know what troubles me, I can only say that I'm your friend through much pity and much fondness, through love. But I can't accept your utopia, nor can I reject it, for I believe that utopia itself is the only possible truth, and something new, and not just a second-hand commodity that is cooked and recooked by human self-interest. You can rely on my friendship, but don't ask for my complicity. Nor can you ask me to follow your ideas along the way if I cannot be sincere.'

'Fine,' I said, 'for me, that's enough. It means we can be friends and can talk. I've now seen you and we have talked, after four months of not talking to anyone. And now I can say goodbye and return home in peace.'

'Not yet,' Liborio said. 'Please stay, you can at least eat with me. I'm alone here, you're my first visitor. You can help me put the house in order, then we can cook and eat together.'

'Agreed,' I said. 'Tell me what to do.'

We went along the bare corridor to his kitchen. The kitchen and three rooms that were his, with another room for a cellar and storeroom, were worse, more dilapidated, than my own house. In each room there was a bare crucifix or other religious image. Liborio had just a bed, a prayer stool, chest, table, several chairs, the kitchen sink, an enamel washbasin. Another chest was full of books, his prized poetry and religious books, among which were pictures of dead saints, photographs of dead ancestors, a few petals, several letters from his parents, then gospel verses and poems, more books, and pictures of the vanity of vanities. These things so dear to poor Liborio were in their chest, on that dusty floor, and I felt as if I had opened a tomb. I told Liborio that he, the parish priest of Acquaviva, should go stealing, should cheat his neighbour in every way, should abuse wives and deflower daughters, snatch money from the charity box, forge wills, compel parishioners to make donations and to bring offerings of gold, silver, jewellery.

'Do you think that's the way to serve this society against which you tell me to fight?' Liborio asked. 'Do you think that's the best way to serve it? You follow your ideas, let me follow mine. I won't even ask you to abandon yours, nor will I teach you how to put them into practice, regardless of my duty as a priest. I won't even tell you to fight against your own pride, even though I often think it's unfounded, for I often considered your science and your studies to be lacking.'

I told him penitently that he was right, and I was wrong. I asked what we would be eating. He said he had some bread, cheese, sausages, and a blood pudding. He kept them in a small zinc food safe.

'As for my ideas,' I continued, 'I'll do exactly what you won't do!'

Outside the church, just behind it, I found some hens belonging to a pious devotee of Saint Anthony. I strangled two of them and returned to Liborio. We sat down, one in front of the other, and plucked them. We then slit them open, each doing his own. We cleaned them, washed them in the sink, then put them to boil. While we were cooking the broth, he said his prayers and I took out one of his books of poetry. I felt strength in that house with that poor priest.

'If you really did what I suggested—stealing, extortion, oppression—but did it with much conviction and much violence, not trying to hide it from anyone, least of all yourself, and if you did it with such violence that you left a trail of violence behind you, like a wolf, then some part of this society would certainly crack, so that some glimmer of a doubt, some small good, might come out of it. Then you'd be a better priest and be of more help to your fellow humans—more help than your prayer and devotion. Forget your church services, rampage through the countryside, begin the slaughter. I'd help you, the two of us could form the most terrifying gang that has ever been through these parts. We should start by waging war on those in power, the landowners, your bishops and cardinals. You could do it with impunity, proclaiming that those villains had been killed by their own arrogance and by the judgement of God. We could hurtle through like a fireball, reform everything, and on your return from each campaign you could stand in the pulpit preaching hellfire sermons. You could say how baseness and authority tremble in the face of violence and vanish when the shadow of death appears. We could demolish and rebuild the cemetery, or eliminate it altogether, and we could use the wealth that once belonged to the wicked to plan and open a great public marketplace, a school, a library, and a children's nursery, a hall for debates, entertainment, dancing, for families to meet, and a building for lectures, for scientific demonstrations, and every other kind of experiment.'

'Do please stop,' Liborio said. 'I already serve one who was cast out, precisely because he sought to fight against those in power. I became a priest to show that power and oppression do not exist and that consciences are free and immovable even in the face of death. Your argument is violence, pointless violence, it's no longer the argument of a scientist, as if your ideas had already lost their direction and you were struggling to choose which path to take. Try to give meaning to your ideas, think carefully about how they can be developed. Don't get carried away, don't involve yourself in projects that are senseless and hateful. I'll tell you now that I have always admired you precisely because you've never complained about being persecuted, and because your only defence or attack has always been through your belief, never any argument that wavered from that. Don't go too far. This discussion of ours is now turning into a childish game.'

'That's not true,' I said. 'You're the child. I seriously think that death might serve me very well to improve my projects, or rather no, to improve, remove, drown in the ditches, bury underground the hateful obstacles and impediments that hinder my projects, not because they're my projects, since they belong to everyone, to be expanded and stretched over the earth like a meadow. So in the face of this hope that stirs me so deeply, I'm not afraid of overcoming some obstacles such as the death of a few thugs or the remorse of a few pusillanimous individuals.'

'I have to tell you,' Liborio said, standing up, 'that your pride has exceeded all bounds, and might end you in disaster.'

'Why do you see pride in these words?' I asked. 'They are just words, which can be changed, as well as being stopped, or even wiped out. But I must always have my ideas, and must never let them weaken, neither within me nor outside, especially now, at the start of a crucial year, during which I intend to take my arguments to their conclusions. I'm not afraid of pride, for I know how to control it better than my hands—and have always kept it within the four walls of my room like a rag ball. And you know that the urge to attack, which can come from my pride, is as tender as an onion shoot and ends up bending on itself, and then returning inside me. Until that moment I, myself, was therefore the testing ground for every experiment of mine. I've never had any compensation or outlets. I have raised my hand to slap my wife only a few times, though I did it knowing that the one to suffer most would be me. And yet, despite this, as you've said, I have never cried out like a victim, and I've never dragged my complaints through the law courts or told my stories in the bars. But, at this point, I'm close to reaching some decisions, and it's right I should reach them consciously, and should bring this consciousness to the extent of my whole knowledge, to the extent of my own feelings and my own imaginings, as far as exploring whether not only the substance of my predictions is possible but the rivulets of their consequences too.'

Liborio stood and asked me to follow him. In the other room, he invited me to sit at the table and brought in the cooking pot. We drank plenty of broth, in silence, and after the third ladle, Liborio lifted out the two chickens and divided them. He paused before he cut the meat, guilty for having forgotten his prayers. He knelt and prayed aloud, also for me, then returned to his chair. We ate our chickens, casting frequent glances at each other, smiling, but said no more. We had no wine and carried on drinking our broth.

At the end, Liborio stood up. With his gleaming pallor, he told me there were several things he had to do. I said goodbye and invited him to visit me. At my house, I said, I would let him read my treatise. He thanked me and as I was leaving, said that he'd help me so far as he could to make peace with Massimina.

I crossed the grass behind the church and returned step by step along the path I had taken that morning. There was the same sun, the same air and nothing had changed, altered only by a half-turn. As I left the houses of Acquaviva, I was no longer worried about the people who lived there, nor afraid of meeting anyone, and I had no regrets. When I reached the bridge, I was struck by the coldness of the breeze and felt an aching that remained not just on my hands and my ears but went deep inside to wake and clothe my disappointment. The disappointment was not about Liborio but about me. I almost envied Liborio, not because he was a priest or because he was fairly strong, but for what lay in front of me, for that surge of friendship and warmth that I felt for him. I envied someone who could be admired and loved by me. The statuette came to mind, and almost into my hands, and it saved me from despair, convincing me that my ideas were already inside me, and I still had to explore them all, and that maybe their results were close, and that nonetheless, even if I never achieved the results, my ideas would still be essential and radiant, since they were founded on the true substance of matter and its laws, and were a consequence of these laws, which I had been able to deduce through the advantage of many circumstances, through the composition of my body and my life and through my own merit. Even if I was now alone and even if I had sunk into my own solitude, this didn't mean that my ideas would also sink.

As I was walking and consoling myself, I heard sounds that had not been there in the morning, so that several times I had to clap my hands. There were many sparrows in groups of four or five, which flew far between one patch of undergrowth and another, between one tree and another, in a radius which was very wide for sparrows. They often stopped and fluttered around me as if to keep me company and landed on the brambles, already hopeful and no longer frightened of the winter. Following the sparrows, I seemed to reach home quickly, and when I arrived under the oak trees and began to see the clumps of ivy on the other part of my land behind them, I realized the day was coming to an end. Sadness greeted me over this boundary.

I moved closer, and the house seemed suddenly weighed down by so many shadows and by so many doubts as if, somewhere inside, something that I myself did not know but had always had was disappearing. No message would arrive and nothing, nothing at all, from that bleak and overcast sky that lay motionless above my desolate house would come down for me and then move before me to explain the operation of the mechanism.

I went up to my room and took the statuette and, after I had placed it on the table, took out the treatise and began to reread it, then wrote down: *Indulgence, i.e. pleasure, indulgence, i.e. the pleasure of being yourself; satisfaction and fear for your own destiny; admiration and friendship—which can be signs of weakness and servitude—are serious dangers. You have to react to these in some way, even desperately, otherwise you can sink into respecting institutions and into the ineptitude of tradition.* Then, without writing anything else, I admitted to myself that I really would react and that my reaction would always be the assertion of my conscience and not some kind of acceptance of defeat, such as escape or suicide; that even if I were to decide to put an end to myself, I would have to behave with the kind of coldness and determination used in an assassination: I would kill myself and would do so because I considered myself to be inefficient, my ideas unwieldy and partially compromised by an uncontrollable mechanism.

I put the treatise aside and started gouging into the statue, by which I mean that I started making a hole in the back of the statuette and through this hole to extract the metal of its substance. I spent many days without ever leaving the house. Hunting and thieving were impossible because wherever I moved, I left tracks and made more noise than a pig in a maize field. Animals now had a strength that I no longer had, for I was giving up and melting away, along with those months of February and March and along with everything, sky and earth, and sank into the muddy ground that swelled up and contaminated everything, even the March stars, even the March ducks that flew high in the sky. They climbed up, altered their course, and I sank. And so I stayed at home for whole days, and ate what resprouted in the vegetable patch, over the superabundance of earth, and olives and walnuts still in the storehouses. I had a few pieces of pig fat and a few pork bones behind Massimina's belongings in the wardrobe and found a clutch of eggs in one corner of the wine cellar.

In mid-March a bitter wind began to blow, freezing everything, halting the growth of the earth. I could go out now, though I had to dart behind trees that had been surprised by the frost, bleeding as they felt their first buds and first flowers torn, the tender joints of many, the more generous and confident, split. I tramped over the metallic earth, buffeted here and there, and saw the roofs of my neighbours' houses stretch and sound, they too, like sheets of ice. I felt revived by this weather, though I gained little from it. It gave me only the chance to go out again, to get a few supplies and to talk to people. They were perhaps intimidated by the sudden change of season and by the persistence of that blustery March wind, so they spoke to me with no contempt and no hostility. They looked at me indeed as though I might have some explanation. They even offered me work, and some invited me to their homes. I accepted these invitations and went to some farmers' houses, to some evening gatherings that were very strange, out of time and out of season, during which no one spoke or watched or sat by the fire, and no one sang or played.

And then from the windows, in that awkward situation in which everything was fixed and arid, about to shatter and fall like a pane of glass, the glimmer of that March front arrived relentlessly and forever: a clear light appeared which did not turn. Everyone looked away in silence from the flames of the hearth or the huddle of their group, towards that light and towards the window, and no one attempted or thought to go and close the shutters, to try to shield themselves from that invasion.

But even when I was alone, standing spellbound at the windows of my house, I had no expectation that something might change, something fundamental, one of the central mechanisms, through an intervention that might come from somewhere else, from the sky, or from another planet. When I was in company, I too was gripped by the fear that something might suddenly change and that mankind was destined to suffer some physical catastrophe—that there would suddenly be no air to breathe, or some poisonous dust from the decomposition of other stars would fall to earth, or that a fire suddenly burned everything up, or that ice came down and froze everything white and blue, so that the white and blue of that March would never be followed by a green April.

But as soon as I abandoned human company, I also abandoned these fears, and kept watching how the days tried to turn colour, prevented by the blocks of white that the wind had accumulated over Petrara and Monlione; and I saw how, day by day, San Savino and all the lands around dwindled more and more in that dry light. It was the crust of the earth itself that seemed to lose its substance and its matter, beneath the atmosphere that lacked the fertility of its corpuscles, its buds, its pollens, and all other contamination.

I tried to think about these phenomena as I noted them down in the margin of my treatise, but couldn't get them completely clear, couldn't understand all their reasons, couldn't glean their purpose.

Meanwhile I continued emptying the statuette and had already made a hole that would take three measures of gunpowder.

March ended with no sign of change, and the air grew heavier and started to carry some infection. On the edges of my fields, towards the woods, some rabbits reappeared with red eyes, and I also heard some hens clucking. One day, as they were clucking, Liborio arrived, on foot like a farmhand.

'I've come to return your visit,' he said, 'to spend the day with you. I see your doors still need repairing and see your fields and vegetable patch abandoned. Today we can start taking down the doors. Over the next day or two we can get on with other jobs since I hope to come back several times.'

'That's fine by me,' I said, 'but first, if you make a start, I'll go and get some food, for the next few days too!'

I invited him inside and left him in the kitchen. I went to get my gun and filled my pockets with cartridges, feeling a sudden glee, thinking how I'd no longer need the gunpowder for that other project, and how I could spend the day and the next few days on a great shooting spree, for my neighbours too, and with my shots I could break that last window in the April sky that I hadn't managed to crack.

I hurried into the woods and started shooting at rabbits. I took a few straight shots at doves or greenfinches that were twittering and flapping from one oak to another. The woods turned into sudden mayhem, and I no longer knew which way to aim since everything was moving, even the top of a juniper or the belly of a broom bush seemed worth a shot. I left the woods and went back up through the fields of vetch that I had left unharvested, between the long lupin spurs and ears of flax that grew among them. There was also much sedge and barley. The hens could stay there in the middle, like partridges, and had learned to use their wings again. I found several of them at the edge of the field where heaps of maize and sorghum stalks lay abandoned for over a year. The hens strutted off and I shot them with the last of the cartridges I had bought from the store. By the time I had filled a sack of rabbits and hens, I realized that in my sudden happiness and in the excitement of the hunt, I had sweated like a child and felt how the air was warmer and the clouds had set into motion, and midday was approaching with its buzz of insects and a calmness that is momentarily suspended in silence as the rope of every bell is lifted. I ran back to my friend Liborio and let him see what I had for him. He had been taking down the doors of the house and cellar and, though still breathless on his feet, with his usual pallor, looked stronger with his sleeves rolled up.

'Your visit is a cause for celebration,' I said, 'and for this celebration, I've been carried away but now promise that we'll work together. I'll take these to one of the neighbours to be cooked.'

That was what I did and was soon back with Liborio. But Liborio didn't want to work with me, preferred that we each worked alone in separate rooms, talking through the wall, not seeing each other. By one o'clock we had already taken much outside to be repaired and worked out what was left to mend.

'This house must have a more welcoming feel,' Liborio said, 'if you want a wife to set foot in here. Just think how a woman wanders around these rooms, goes to these cupboards, closes the windows, leans on the windowsill, sweeps the floors, washes the steps, and how you hear her walking about upstairs, or in the store-houses, and in the bedroom, shaking the bedsheets and singing. My dear Anteo, try to be worthy of that gift of love.'

'Have you had any news of Massimina?' I asked.

'Well, yes,' Liborio said, 'I was going to tell you in the next day or so. I hear she'll be back in her village for Easter—if not Easter, then certainly the Sunday after.'

I was pleased to hear this but disturbed by the fact that it was Liborio who had told me. I was disturbed not so much by Liborio's voice and his generosity—which, like all generosity, seemed like a sacrifice for him and somehow also for me—but because Massimina would be returning so soon, for Easter, which was barely three weeks away. This unease dampened my enthusiasm, and the work before me no longer seemed like a spontaneous invention but a pretext.

It was a sad revelation. Liborio's visit and what he had told me was sad, and it was sad that the two of us wouldn't have so much time to spend working and chatting, each perhaps in their own room. This mixture of feelings remained with me over lunch, which we spent at the house of a woman who lived nearby and had prepared a lavish meal. Afterwards, in front of the fire, while Liborio moved his pallid figure to one side to keep the heat away from his face, all my feelings were transformed into the strongest urge to embrace a woman, perhaps because I saw this neighbour lean forward two or three times to blow on the fire and move away with a look of radiance, and, in my thoughts, this woman had become Massimina, with her narrow eyes and her moles, even though her body was different, less precise.

When it was time to say goodbye, Liborio said, 'Look, no one's going to warn Massimina, no one's going to say anything on your behalf. I'm sure she'll come back. Go and see her, talk to her, but no one's going to arrange any meeting and no one's going to tell her family to stop it from happening. Try to keep calm and work, and prepare yourself as if it were some test that Massimina is expecting, or a test she herself has arranged. Just try to arrange everything as if Massimina were coming back to your house that Sunday after Easter. Take these words not as some promise or prediction but as a firm intimation of hope.'

I spent the next few days arranging for work to be done in my fields and hired two tractors for the heavier jobs. I still had some money and could make a good impression on my neighbours and on traders. Liborio came back and did some more work for a few days, mainly in the house, going up and down, appearing at the windows every now and then. I was most unsure and gazed at my statuette, which now had the hole in its back.

The days didn't share my uncertainty, for they passed one after another, ever brighter and ever busier; each hill and each field fully back in place, blooming and covering and encouraging the others around: together they were once more the hills of San Savino, below the crags of Monlione and above the valleys of Acquaviva. The colours were the same each day, especially in the evening, and since the sky warmed from the day, everything at dusk was red and purple and the coloured circle expanded more each evening, and in a few days that step would be as wide as the entry of summer. Even the farmers stopped to gaze at the spectacle of these occurrences, and were pleased, and accepted the warmth that came down and the billowing blossom of each plant and each tree; they too came out touched by these things and conveyed their fervour and indeed passed it from one hill to the other, along with the braying of the donkeys. I looked much at nature, for I always had my scientific thought in mind, even though I had once again abandoned it; but it was always there, like a basil plant on my windowsill. And just like basil, I could always catch its scent.

My position insofar as nature is clear and comes from my scientific thought. It has never been one of submission and obedience, nor one of rejection or indifference, even if I think nature itself has to be transformed like the surface on which another life can move. And yet during those days, my position was not so clear and I—who have always trusted the things around me following my view of them, trusting even those things that are viewed as non-essential and regarded as mechanisms outdated and to be replaced—began to feel a sense of betrayal towards nature. I began to feel something that I couldn't accurately describe and which that evening, after considering it several times, I could only explain as being part of the destiny of my neighbours, as distress at the deception that nature was practising on them once more, and the poor, unknowing meekness with which they fell into this deception, the same, exactly the same, for so many years, which always had the same allurements, which never even needed to change its course.

And nature proceeded with its days growing brighter and a little larger, one after another, like so many siblings, until that Easter day arrived, in late April, on all the olive leaves, willow tips and oak branches, which now assumed their colour and their nobility.

There had been a few prompt and decorous downpours of rain which had flattened all the flowers and reopened every spring in the earth. I too was billowing and quivering like a willow, waiting to meet Massimina, and was moved by the thought of all that would happen and how exactly I would hear of her return and where I would meet her alone, since it would be hard to face the eyes of the whole village on Easter day, meeting her from church. Or it would be easier to meet her together with the others and emerge from the crowd as the one who was chosen and predestined, who takes one step forward, striding confidently unlike the others, and shouldering the trepidation of all the others and their greetings.

Liborio had no more to tell me at the right moment, and spoke only briefly, at the far end of his church, which was even colder than in wintertime, with its doors wide open and some meagre bunches of flowers lost in a few drops of yellow water in a jar. I thought Liborio looked sad at the sight of his poor church and its walls, below which it was hardly enough to place three bunches of primroses. His sadness might then have been caused by the predominance of all around us in that season, after the privations of winter, sparking a sadness in that state in which we look around bewildered, expecting nature, humanity, and everything else—ourselves and our own feelings—to assume a more precise appearance and tone.

In that condition, I—who did not give up easily and did not calm my restlessness with the distraction of work or by going off to pick flowers—became as uncertain as a child, ended up mirroring myself in some other thing, finding a mirror always in front of me, and this mirror was never obliging but was each time vague and therefore cruel.

I spent the eve of Easter day with Liborio and returned with this uncertainty and with these mirrors. Fortunately, on my way home, having left the more rugged ground, closer to the hill and therefore behind it, where it was still frosty, I found the fields fairly well advanced and promising after the recent work that had been carried out.

I passed a fairly peaceful night at home, spending the first half going around checking that each bedroom, the kitchen, and storehouses were in order. In every room, there was a strong smell of paint and whitewash which permeated the whole house.

Next morning, I got up and dressed. I didn't want to go looking about inside or out, so consoled myself by pulling out the statuette, looked at it, put it on the kitchen table.

I hurried through the rooms, shut the doors, and rode off on the motorcycle I had borrowed. I kept my eyes on the road towards Serra Sant'Abbondio and Doglio, and kept my thoughts to myself, ignoring the air and all those things that moved around me which might catch my attention and distract my mind and could therefore prompt many thoughts. But something still touched me, still passed through my mind to reach my senses, even my heart: a dove in flight, or a flattened broom bush, or a stone, or water gushing into a drain, or the cut of a straw stack, or nothing—for I was sometimes surprised by something I could no longer find when I expected to see it. I tried to keep to myself, conceding nothing, and meanwhile stored up all those things that came to watch me and tried to keep me company.

I crossed behind Montevecchio for Serra Sant'Abbondio without passing through Doglio, as though I were frightened of carrying such thoughts into one of those chasms or nests of thorns of which Doglio is made.

I reached Serra and lit a cigarette in the middle of the piazza. I walked up and down between the piazza and the church and could see none of Massimina's family. I saw none of them, neither she nor her family, at any of the masses up to midday. So as not to go hungry, I rode to the store at the sulphur mine. I came back to Serra, but still saw no one, so went straight to Doglio, to the house of the first of the three ambassadors. I didn't knock but passed the door three times. I rode around again, as far as the Doglio church and the sanctuary, then went back to Serra and stood again in the piazza. I rode towards the Frontone road, further down where couples would go walking and where it was warmer and there were more meadows and more hedges. I then went to look at Massimina's house but could see it was shut and empty.

I went back the following Sunday and took the same roads in the same way. This time everything around was as if cut in half, and I was conscious of just the beginning or the end, or the contours. Not even my anxiety nor my suffering were whole within me. Everything happened as if some invisible being beside me were preventing me from seeing and touching and ordering things, as if my machine had lost some of its power and was still working, but with much grinding and grating.

That Sunday was also very dull, overcast, and there were few people about. I managed to summon my strength, to tell myself to expect no sadness. I didn't know a black cloud was about to cross the solar system. I thought I had spent too long alone. For too long my studies had brought no results, not even for myself.

I went back to my motorcycle intending to take the shortest route back to San Savino. When I reached the bend by the cemetery, just after the slope, I saw Massimina climbing down to the road from a gulley where there was no path, looking at the ground, choosing her step.

She turned pale when she saw me and her eyes looked anxious. I said hello, still sitting on the motorcycle gazing at the ground behind her, at the steep rugged banks and ditches, rather than at her. She stopped and looked up, trying as best she could to reach the same level and to get away. She stepped back to find a metre of flat road beneath her heels.

'Here we are again,' I said.

'Yes,' she said, 'after you chose to abandon me.'

'You know that's not true.'

'How should I know?'

'Well,' I said, 'try at least to think about what I tell you, and you can see whether you think it's true and whether you agree.'

'Oh, I don't want to argue. But I'll tell you now, I'm going back to Rome tomorrow. That's where my life is, where I can look after myself without too much upset.'

'The road from here to Rome is shorter than you think,' I said. 'That's not enough by itself to answer our problems, nor to take away the upset, if it's real.'

'What problems?' she asked.

'The problem at least that you and I should be living together.'

'No!'

'Why not?'

'No,' she repeated. 'You even reported me to the police, made me run the risk of ending up before a judge.'

'I'm the one who's judging you,' I said.

'Your judgement makes no sense. Every judgement you ever make is against your own interest, as well as the interests of those who cared for you.'

'My judgement is crystal clear, and isn't formed on the hatred of all those people around you. My judgement towards you has always been the love I hold for you.'

'Beaten into me?'

'The beatings are irrelevant, and you know that. You know they're something else, something different, not even real, which didn't even happen. Please listen to me, for what I have to say now is that your love, and your closeness, they matter more even than my science.'

'Your science is no more than an obsessive madness.' she sighed. 'Your intelligence is twisted, you use it against your own interest, against everyone's interest. I don't understand where you get this madness. Looking at you, even sometimes being with you, people wouldn't say you were mad!'

'I don't want to talk about my science,' I said. 'Not because you can't understand or because it's something that's different from us and can even work against us. But in this moment, I repeat, my science means less than my love. I want to live with you, like I want to embrace you. San Savino would be full again if you were back with me, or we could go to Rome together, or live on the coast.'

197

I moved towards Massimina and took her by the arm. She turned her head towards me, looking up, her eyes glowering. Her cheek was pale and under her ears I could see a veil of face powder. I took her in both arms and squeezed her flesh above her elbows, almost falling and putting my weight onto my legs which were still supporting the motorcycle. I abandoned the tone of argument and moved my whole self towards her. I moved near to her face.

'Where are you going now?' I asked.

'Why, where can I go?' she replied.

'Down there, even,' I said, pointing to the rear of a hedge below the road embankment.

'What does that mean?'

'For me, it means everything.'

'For you . . . do what you like, but you must let me free.'

'You are free, you can do what you like. I just ask you now to come and live with me, and to decide then for our whole life.'

'That answer doesn't mean a lot,' she said. 'If I live with you, then you'll let me go?'

'Yes, I'll let you go.'

'But you'll no longer search for me if I go off to Rome?'

'But what do you want—that I go searching for you or not?'

'I want you to leave me in peace,' she said.

'But this peace, you think you'll get it without me? Or do you think we might have a more beautiful peace, together?'

'Don't test me,' she said, 'just accept that my answers are also made with the help of those who want to protect me.'

'All right,' I said, 'I'll leave you free to do as you wish, but that doesn't mean I'll let you go, because I love you.'

I kissed Massimina and led her down. She offered no resistance and followed me, propping herself on me. 'If you want to obtain some satisfaction,' she said. She didn't show her sadness even when I put my arms around her and kissed her. She was ready, instead, with her coat undone. I held her tightly and kissed her and, with my tongue on her face, I felt a taste that was different from that of the Massimina who had come to my house, but my longing for her was now so strong that I could feel no anger, nor could I defend my love from my own longing!

'This is violence, what you're doing to me,' she said, but her submissiveness in every gesture was so full and so complete, even in her nakedness, which was more than mere compliance and seemed to be her true substance, as she exposed her stomach and turned her head slightly or opened a leg. And she did these things, semi-clothed, with an intimacy that poured down and was gently lost as if it were some natural occurrence. I loved everything about her and repeated my love, frantically. In the end, she smiled to herself, and this smile became fixed for a while as she attempted to dry and cover herself, among those garlands of briars that turned blue as the night fell. I too felt a great coldness and could hear a trickle of spring water behind us that had not been there before. The coldness and the night frost suddenly fell upon my face and upon hers, and upon our moist mouths. I moved close to her again and covered her once more, as if to warm and protect her. On this last time, so complicated and fateful, I had a deeper sense of everything within me, and around me, and in Massimina, whose frame was slimmer and warmer, and I relaxed gently to her breath. Many words then came to me that were different from my own, and I asked her to return, that evening, to my house, and to stay with me forever. Massimina made no reply and hugged me and gripped my head so hard that it hurt me, while she gazed into the air, blankly, as if she were searching for an answer among those two stars. But she uttered not a single word.

When I stood up, my teeth were chattering from the cold and my legs were quivering. Massimina was also in a bad way, apart from her eyes, and walked with her legs splayed, uncomfortably. I walked with her along the entire road and at the sight of the first houses I wanted to move close to her, but she pushed me away and said, 'This further proof, I don't think it counts.'

'What proof?' I asked.

'I'm leaving for Rome tomorrow because I'm not coming back with you. These places now, they're not for the two of us. But I'll not leave you without hope, so I'll ask His Excellency to pass your letters on to me if you want to write. Now I must go, immediately. I don't want to regret what I've done and fall into despair.'

I stopped and let her walk on alone. 'I'll write straightaway,' I said, 'but I want a reply. You'll see in my letters that you'll find the strength you don't have now. Sorry if I've weakened you, it wasn't what I wanted! I'm feeling weaker myself, but I'm sure tomorrow, just thinking about you, I'll get my strength back, and I'll write the first letter. Believe me, Massimina, don't be frightened of my science, it's a good companion. Don't be frightened of anyone.'

'Goodbye,' she said.

I thought, the next morning, about Massimina's train to Rome and thought it would have been better and safer if I had taken her in Rome rather than Serra Sant'Abbondio, had taken her from His Excellency's house in Via Uruguay. I felt a nostalgia for Rome and seemed to hear the clatter of the train on its descent from Fabriano, as it rumbled below the cliffs of Fossato and over the bridges between Nocera to Foligno. It was a nostalgia for somewhere wide and flat, teeming with people who had no fixed place or way of life.

My nostalgia for Rome turned into a yearning after those letters I wrote each week to Massimina in which I described my hopes and spoke of love. I thought about that meeting with her on the Sunday after Easter and regretted each time that I hadn't enjoyed it from the very start, hadn't taken proper account of every moment of love, of Massimina's presence, her body, her clothing, her beating heart. As I wrote these letters, I was seized each time by a longing for her and to hold her straightaway, and I described what I felt and how I thought of her, and I kept that sheet of paper on the table.

When my feelings subsided and the letter was finished and sealed, this was the moment when my nostalgia for Rome came, and I started thinking about the letter arriving, the post offices from whose doors it might leave on its way to Via Uruguay, and I thought about the trolley buses that left San Silvestro every half hour for Via Uruguay. In this way I seemed to see Rome again and recalled the piazzas that I knew and the road junctions from which

I walked to the university or Porta Portese and then, more exactly, a longing to be back on Viale dell'Università, on my way for an appointment with a professor, and could see the stairs I had climbed, and saw them as if for the first time, in that moment, and had not yet been turned away, in other words, as if my hopes were still intact and I were climbing those stairs on my way to present my treatise.

June and July are long months, they give no respite, and my feelings of nostalgia tormented me, not least because Massimina did not reply and I seemed to hear the continual rumbling, behind the mountains, of convoys of people on their way to Rome. I tried to work on my treatise but made little progress and spent much of the night watching the stars and saw many that fell, abandoned by their automaton-creators, or moved to conquest, or to the academy of other planets. I was stuck at the chapter on *The integrity of automatic dynamisms*, also because I could no longer find the proposition from which I had set out to show this integrity. Perhaps I had thought of a perpetual and inextinguishable model, which had then collapsed and which I could no longer distinguish from the platform of the real world and from the mixture of things I was observing. I searched in my mind for the hypothesis by which in biological processes, as well as in those natural processes that seemed more rigid and are merely repeated, evolution has a significant function, so that none of these processes is ever the same as the one before.

How had I therefore managed to establish the proposition of the integrity of automatic dynamisms? I sometimes feared that having claimed this integrity meant also having admitted it to myself, and therefore having posited the principle of a faith, of a fixed and fundamental cornerstone, or a pre-established divinity that might even have upset the totality and the impetus of the creative uncertainty of my science and its constant freedom, even in front of the description, the weight and the position of bodies. I could not begin to undermine my position by accepting that something was integral and had to remain integral: even if this were the function of automatic dynamisms—that is, the repetition of movements and the integration of these movements into the sphere of the world machine.

I really feared that I had forsaken something for my love of Massimina, my friendship towards Liborio, and my solitude, and was no longer trembling in the way that the problem in front of me at that moment required me to, namely, the problem of the uncertainty of science, seen as the uncertainty and therefore as the instrument, the language, and the art of a continual becoming in the progress of the academy of friendship; all the more since uncertainty relates to the particles, the bodies, and the smallest details, above all those minuscule details, those that are moved by an invisible discharge of automaton-creators, those that float through the whole universe and as far as touching the ground on which we think, our brain and our cells. Altogether, these minuscule bodies, stimuli, and events form—more than the falling of celestial bodies or the changing of the seasons—the great liquid currents that will change the world. Therefore, since nothing is fixed, nothing can be described as an integral and rigid mechanism in the banal concatenation of causes and effects.

The purpose of science is to help us express ourselves in the best possible way and therefore to correct us and to change us to the point of reforming every pre-existing law and form. None of the contents of these laws and forms is therefore sacrosanct.

When, towards the end of July, having succeeded in bringing my treatise to the firm conclusion that I have stated, I was about to yield to a moment of exhaustion, a letter arrived from Massimina:

'Anteo, I have received your letters and have opened and read them, even if I sometimes had to stop reading some of them that went too far. I haven't always understood everything you said, nor do I understand how you can love me as you say and behave in another way and still cut yourself off, not working, throwing your life away, which is the greatest sin of all and just proves that you're not interested in your own life and therefore you're not interested in the life of others. What love is this? But I can't spend too much time writing because it upsets me, because I can't forget how you appeared in my life, how we lived together, and then how we broke up. All those shattered hopes and your strangeness and wickedness have destroyed me, right up to the last one, which was the way you behaved when we met at Serra. While you are thinking about love, I'm in trouble, and am waiting with much fear. You also say to wait, so that's what we're doing, my family too, and must carry on doing, now that we've set things in motion that we can no longer stop, and we must wait until they reach the end. We have also put the law into action, and the law goes on, and it no longer depends on what we want, and will reach its conclusion for us. I pray God also to be freed once more from the fear that has been torturing me over the last few days, that your violence might bring me some other fruit, which would be the most unjust of all, and which it kills me even just to think about. Don't write again. Tomorrow we're off to the coast. I'll write when I return if I'm feeling better. Goodbye, Massimina.'

I went on living and watching the stars, and every so often I had a sudden attack which shook me, which convulsed my brain. I began thinking of the impossibility of proving anything, for example, that a tree or a star could exist just the same at one moment after the other. I was therefore gripped by a determination in which I admitted repeatedly, mechanically, that uncertainty proves evolution, just as evolution proves uncertainty, and therefore that science can be none other than uncertainty and evolution, and that since uncertainty is none other than the instrument for communicating, for touching, for moving forward, and since evolution is the stimulus for improving and believing that everything must strive to become better than what it is until . . . To wait therefore, even in science, as Massimina said: for me to wait too. I thought about it during the day, but almost only to accept without much conviction that to wait, for me, certainly didn't mean to suffer more or less, as it did for Massimina, whom I loved just the same, or for her family. In any event, a relentless destiny, and then the end as an exact and natural conclusion of a death already constructed minute by minute, in the acquiescence of all the days spent in a life that made it impossible to live, in other words, to evolve and improve and to break at any moment anything that tended to become established in spite of itself, whether it were a form or a law or a society . . .

Meanwhile I harvested in a very haphazard fashion and didn't have much of a yield from it. My situation was in fact worse because I had spent all my money on ploughing and sowing and was left with just a few hundred kilos of grain and a useless stack of hay. I still had to harvest the maize and pick the grapes, and therefore had to run into further debt. Selling the grain meant further pointless labour, winnowing it, putting it into sacks, transporting it to Cagli. I didn't even go asking Liborio for help.

Then, in mid-September, the summons arrived to appear at the court in Pergola. I went. They were summary proceedings, and I was dealt with in two hours. The witness statements were those I set out at the beginning of this book.

Back home I found a letter from Massimina. The paper inside was covered with marks that looked deliberate, made as if to frighten me, and was unsigned, where I had to read this:

'Anteo, cruel brute, you've done it deliberately to ruin me, with your hopeless love. You've ruined me for ever, completing your work with your final stroke of genius; but I pray God that you pay for everything. All you've ever given me is the suffering of an animal. Now I must die but I pray God to live just long enough to know that your sins have devoured you. What else can be said by someone who must die, through your fault? I am the wretched woman you have ruined.'

Only my treatise could protect me and comfort me, for my love brought me only pain and was more indulgent than a grievous illness. I tried always to have it in front of me or in my hands, never to be without it, not even for a moment, and never to lose heart in the languor of October.

I made no attempt to arrange anything that might save me from Massimina's accusations and from the ruin she had sworn to bring upon me and had unleashed against me, for it seemed pointless as well as too painful, and I'd have been forced once again to examine my wounds.

In November I received the summons for the appeal case in Urbino. I was waiting for this hearing to present my explanations, which never left me and followed me everywhere, since they were a living part of me, and couldn't be buried in the past. Every now and then, against these explanations, I could feel beneath my tongue the cruel hope of seeing Massimina again, and the even crueller hope that the hearing might serve to bring about a public reconciliation after she had declared her guilt to the judges and unmasked the plot organized against me.

On the appointed day, I left for Urbino before dawn. It was snowing when I went to catch the bus and I had no coat. I kicked the snow away as lightly as if it were confetti, for nothing had to stop me, and I had no concern even for the things around me.

But the snow brought the bus to a halt below Urbino, then it started moving slowly like inside a barrel vault. Overhead were trees weighed down with ice and higher still the mighty construction of the city, first the walls and then the buildings above them.

I was attracted by these buildings, by their great facades, almost all the same, drawn together like one body, and I asked my fellow passenger what they were. He pointed to the nearest building on a lone hill. 'That's the cemetery,' he said, then pointed to the others in a row on the city hill. 'That's the slaughterhouse,' and then the second, 'that's the court building,' the third, 'the hospital,' the fourth, 'the prisons,' the fifth, 'the convent, an enclosed order,' the sixth, 'the church of the dead,' the seventh, 'the police station,' the eighth, 'the university,' and then another convent and the customs house.

'Here's the fine appearance that cities keep for their country-side and their rural folk,' I thought. 'And yet it's fine indeed, and it makes you feel thankful, and even ashamed to be afraid of it.'

Inside, the city was packed as tightly as a walnut and had small piazzas, courtyards, and streetfuls of steps. Along these steps you reached a large white piazza so wind-lashed that the snow was all a gleaming sheet over the cathedral steps and the whole piazza which, at the far end, opened on either side and was called Il gioco-pallone.

An alley from the sheltered side of the piazza led towards the court building. The first doors of the court were open but all those after were closed and covered with green cloth.

The people I saw inside, around the stoves, didn't look like city folk but more like prison warders. Inside, there would be no place for my conscience, nor for my science. I could sniff the hostile odour of those halls and those people, like you can smell a dog. The odour of police capes too. Despite this, I kept my courage and was ready to brook no compromise and never to excuse myself for what I hadn't done. Let justice be done and let us see who must bring it—and be sure, I added, not to let them pull it out ready-made from one of these cabinets and corners.

I was taken into the courtroom and put by a bench.

Massimina wasn't there at the trial and her absence was made sadder still by the presence of her brother, and her younger sister who rather resembled her and wore a coat like hers.

The judge asked if I was familiar with the allegations, and I said no. He then asked why I had ill-treated my wife. I told him that I had never ill-treated Massimina, as she knew deep down, just as the false witnesses also did. What I administered was not ill-treatment when I sought to correct her and when I tried to tell her about my projects and to interest her in my studies, and to persuade her to help me with them.

'What studies?' the judge asked.

'My scientific studies. I'm writing a treatise on creation and rebirth.'

'Ah,' the judge said, 'we have a Galileo!'

'Haven't you reached Einstein yet?' I asked.

'What do you mean? What are you suggesting?' the judge asked. 'If you were a little Galileo, you'd have quite enough to be satisfied about, you'd have our respect and that of society, and you would certainly not have been involved in those matters you are accused of here. I say Galileo in this sense, in the respect and acknowledgement that is due to science. This court will not take your ideas into account and will limit itself to examining and judging the acts you have committed. Do you admit these acts?'

'There are no acts,' I said. 'I have committed no acts, good or bad, because everything, or almost everything, lies beyond science, in the mortal inertia of this nature and of this society; even less is there justice, unless we mean the futile mask of a time and a convention that are dead and buried, fixed and rigid, precisely because they are dead; and such a mask has been placed upon them, precisely because they are dead, to cover time past and the scourges of their death.'

'This argument has no meaning,' said the judge, 'and if I wanted to try giving it one, I'd have to commit you in the end for contempt of court. Keep to the allegations and tell me whether you're aware of having committed these acts, whether you remember them, and whether you admit to having participated, and therefore accept responsibility.'

'I repeat, the allegations do not exist, I have no responsibility. The responsibility is yours, seeing that you wish to give importance to matters that don't exist, that are dust along the road of evolution. If you wish to stop to collect this dust and to start shouting scandal, trying to stop progress or to prevent me from moving along with it, then those responsible for these allegations are you, for at the moment you receive them, fix them, give them substance and importance, you give them life, like a mortal weight.'

'Very well,' said the judge, 'you go ahead with progress. I'll stop to gather the facts, and when I've examined them, I'll catch up with you and maybe I'll stop you along the road, however fast you're going, and this stop might last a few months, and might end up in a prison cell. Who is representing this defendant?'

My lawyer stood up.

'Your Honour already has a clear picture of my client's personality,' he said, 'and will therefore appreciate how this personality has interpreted or coloured these allegations. I ask the court therefore to investigate the defendant's personality and to consider his scientific ideas. Who knows whether they might offer some key to his behaviour. The defendant has indeed stated that his misunderstandings with his wife stem from his attempt to interest her in his doctrines.'

'If your client were charged with murder,' the judge replied, 'then we might perhaps spend time delving into his ideas on creation, but this is a trial for domestic abuse, the facts are clear, and we don't intend to waste any further time. If the defendant won't plead guilty to these allegations and isn't prepared to explain them, then we shall hear the witnesses and can deliver our judgement at the end. Are we going to follow Descartes or lose ourselves in the dialogue on world systems? Are we going to ask Signor Crocioni whether he uses inductive or deductive reasoning? We mustn't end up like Francis Bacon who spent so much time on a scientific experiment that he caught a chill and died!'

I stood up and said: 'You and your fellow judges should, all the same, follow Bacon's method—that of experimentation. And therefore, to measure the facts, you need them to be repeated and you wait for the results, then have them repeated again, and wait for the new results to see if they are the same as before, in such way as to construct an experience that carries a recognized value. But I don't think you could follow the Cartesian method since you've abandoned reason and its charters. You cannot in truth seek inspiration from the rational method, precisely because it eliminates the facts and considers them only as pretexts and consequences of little importance for the exquisite laws of reason. Events are superseded and forgotten, as is right, and all that is left is exquisite reason, which certainly won't produce much of a flicker here. You and your fellow judges are most suited to following Bacon in the most ordinary way and thus, to believe the allegations, you ought to repeat them, and you yourselves should therefore go about ill-treating each other and ill-treating others.

'I cannot therefore tell you to follow me, even if in this way you would find the only road, if you really claim the right to correct and regulate human relations. Then you would be aware that I go beyond even the exquisite law of reason since, as it is, it makes a goddess out of reason, since it never admits to comparison, nor does it consider itself incomplete before the intelligence of science and all its results and phenomena. Not even this goddess is enough for me, and I prefer not to commit myself to anything, moved as I am by my freedom and my purity, on the path of evolution, and for this reason always ready to improve.'

'Fortunately for you, we have no wish to listen to these ravings,' the judge said. 'They have led you to attack even the Church, and the Church has generously chosen not to respond, so as not to ruin you.'

'That's not true,' I answered. 'The Church has tried to ruin me—and succeeded, at least financially.'

'Don't push your arguments too far, nor your own importance,' said the judge. 'Why should the Church cause you financial ruin? Having once ignored your rambling ideas, the Church would have no reason to attack you.'

'Oh yes,' I said, 'several reasons. First, because I'm communist.'

'Ah', said the judge, 'you're a communist too? This seems like another interesting discovery. How can you be a communist if you believe in evolution and difference? What does the party say about your theories?'

'I've never joined the Communist Party and have never discussed my ideas with anyone of importance in the party. But I can see it was a mistake, and as soon as I'm free from this trial, I'll write to Moscow for an invitation to the USSR Academy of Science, as an observer at least, hoping I might present my ideas and the treatise that I'm writing, and discuss them all with the space scientists.'

'How can you say you're a communist?' asked the judge. 'Don't you know you can't be a communist if you're not in the party?'

'That's not true,' I answered, 'I'm communist even if I'm outside the party and have little interest in the party. Nor am I much interested in class war in this chaos deliberately created by the bourgeoisie. I'm communist because, for me, science is the foundation of life and because I recognize science as the only possibility for life. Communist society can never be as rigid as this because it will always follow behind scientific progress and will be constantly updating itself, improving current machines and building others, as it has already begun to do.'

'I have to point out,' said the judge, 'that you're wrong here too in your idea about communist society, since nothing is more rigid than this society and nothing is less scientific than its ideals which reject difference and insult human dignity.'

'I'd rather not continue arguing with you,' I said, 'your words offend me. You have the power and the authority to judge me, so please proceed with this power and authority, but I cannot allow you to call the wrong you're doing me by some other name, re-baptised and distorted, then justified for the sake of the record. Your justification is through power alone.'

'Silence,' said the judge, 'I'm the one who doesn't wish to understand, and in fact I don't understand your words and your ravings!'

The trial went ahead, and the witnesses all gave their evidence against me. The prosecutor addressed the judge.

'I didn't intervene earlier to have this man silenced out of a sense of pity, but above all out of horror. His folly and his criminal action are not human, and such a brazen and insidious impudence is surely the product of a depraved mind, deliberately aimed at the destruction of society . . .'

The lawyer appointed to represent me stood up.

'The key question in this trial,' he said, 'lies in the personality of the defendant who behaves like a paraphrenic. His ideas are the fruit of his folly, consisting essentially, though in their total emptiness, of expressions and nothing more than expressions, of words more or less erratic, impenetrable and confused, the sound of which has fascinated and intrigued their author. His thinking is therefore autistic, consisting of onomatopoeia, assonances, stereo-types, eccentricities.'

'They're not mere words and rhymes,' I said. 'You're the one who doesn't understand!'

'Yes,' my lawyer replied, 'I don't understand your words because your logic is different and, if I may say, infirm . . .'

'No, I'm the one who refuses to understand your words, and to employ the mechanisms that motivate and construct them, for they concern my freedom and the purity of my intentions. You're the ones who are raving, with this trial of yours! And you banter words, and use them and count them, like the tally of points at the end of a card game, and your cards are greasier and dirtier than any cards ever played in any bar room. You don't look outside, you don't use your heads, you have no tongues left, all you have is filthy documents and money. Meanwhile your world floats and falls and will event-ually drop into the hands of others, but you will not then be judged, for none of the victors who arrive will be stupid enough to believe in trials. You will convict yourselves, for your incapacity to under-stand; you will understand nothing, and you will be lost, worse than a poor herd of cattle. You won't even manage to pronounce your names, for your voices will be nothing more than a howl.'

I said these things as I was dragged away from the court by order of the judge. I was sentenced to a year in prison but released straightaway because the sentence was suspended.

I walked down from the court to the piazza, dark and blanketed with thick snow. I found two students under the portico who offered me something to eat and drink and found me a bed in their lodgings.

I went home the next day feeling totally dejected. Before me, clearly expressed in my lawyer's final words, was the whole mass of preoccupations, pain, uncertainties, failings, fears, pride, along with conceit, melancholy, regret, sickness, harboured since the day the three ambassadors had been to visit me, accompanied by a weight that stretched and swelled between my heart and stomach in Rome and then once again in San Savino, as far as those dark courtroom benches in Urbino.

I shut myself in the house and pulled out the statuette. I went back to emptying it, with determination, trying to gouge out as much metal as I could. I had no wish to go hunting and made no attempt to catch the thrushes when they returned to my vegetable patch in December. I opened the doors of my grain store to feed the hens, rabbits, thrushes, blackbirds, and any other innocent animal that was much more of a brother to me than the judge and the lawyer.

The fundamental aspect of the problem that most depressed me was this: 'How can I, alone, ever manage to give sufficient force to my ideas to stir such a poor and degenerate multitude of my fellow creatures? I will never therefore achieve any result, for this result cannot be understood and accepted and will remain just like the trail of a falling star.' My scientific language was now less clear, intermingled with my sorrow and naturalistic impressions of an artistic kind, and when my statuette was almost completely empty and its figure still complete, but as empty as a chalice, I received the final call.

On 11 January 1960, *Il Messaggero* reported the following news:

'Domestic servant in Via Uruguay kills newborn baby, its tiny corpse found in a box beneath her bed.

'Rome, 10 January. A domestic servant from the Marche has been arrested in Via Uruguay, accused of infanticide and conceal-ment of a corpse. The woman, Massimina Meleschi Crocioni, age 29, from Serra Sant'Abbondio (Pesaro-Urbino), was working as a servant with the family of a senior government official when she went into labour in the early hours of 8 January. With remarkable composure she locked herself in the bathroom where she gave birth, removing all trace of what had happened. Crocioni had pre-viously managed to conceal her condition, continuing to work nor-mally with no apparent sign of weakness. The family with whom she was living noticed her state of extreme exhaustion around 1.00 pm while she was serving at table. They also found suspicious traces of blood and called the police. A subsequent search of the maid's bedroom brought to light the tiny corpse of a newborn child under the bed, wrapped in newspaper in a shoe box. Crocioci was admitted to hospital, where she is being kept under guard.'

She ought to have died, and instead she was the killer. All the same, it was against me that she committed this murder, and with the cruellest will, against me on the body of that poor child who hadn't even opened its eyes. How much better if I had closed my eyes, during any of those moments we had spent together, even for a second, so that poisonous snake could have attacked me instead. The image of the poor newborn child remained with me, the holes of its face bound by death, like the most familiar picture I had ever seen, discovered now, but forever etched inside the house, in its bedrooms, on the walls and in the closest lineaments of the earth and sky.

My body then grew rigid, and my mind was cut away from me, my mind and body both deprived of any possibility to act, both isolated, as if every piece had lost any unifying intention and their constructors had returned to freedom, inside and outside, regardless of the snow.

Every so often, my eyes would see my hands, still disconnected and on different plains. Each thing, in the house and out in the countryside, moved closer and further from my senses, of its own accord, with movements over which I had no control or choice. My sight did not guide me, nor did it even stay with me; it functioned over me like a mirror that reflects something that cannot be seen, hidden above the person who is watching. Since I could not choose—nor was I dying—everything inside my house and in the landscape weighed heavily on my sight. Complicated constructions crowded in on me, one over the other, with their structures, so that I seemed to move among a mountain of unsteady forms and objects that risked at any moment to topple down on me and scatter me.

Against the pain I began to drive back the constructions that most offended me, which were not those more pointed constructions towards which I tried to move to be touched but were rounded and oval constructions where the countryside was indulgent and where there was an order, especially in points of contact and in the lines of juncture, which had become my own pain from the first moment in which it had appeared before me—as if it had finally appeared for this reason alone, to bring me sorrow and with the very substance of my pain, which was also spread across the whole countryside, over every object and also in so many other places, and which now began to assemble and to set itself against me, signifying that everything had now established its own order, in perpetual antagonism against me, as if I no longer had meaning and limit, nor body, nor control, and everything everywhere existed against me.

In this oval order that appeared to me, in which rows of vines were joined to lanes, and hills to hills, like eggs on a plate, interspersed every now and then by a large tree or a house, or by an old tower, or by a stream or a lake, or just a single piece of wood that floated, all was as clean as the background of the painting of Saint Sabinus Victorious. I saw in this bright picture that order of things that must have been the cruel order of Massimina, of her family and of everyone, the order where pain is accepted like the blue mantle of sky and where all other existence, love, appetite, friendship, is hidden among the lines of the joints, in the holes, and sucked furtively beneath that sky in which the soul is confounded and all reason is lost, yet to continue the hypocritical perversion of remaining to enjoy their own flesh, avid and sprawling, of sucking the earthly things that are hidden, and making love, and swallowing while they are swallowed up. All then, during each of these libidinous actions, tend to disguise themselves, bury themselves, disavow nature, cover themselves, desiring deep down to raise the margins of the earth in search of the nourishing protection of death.

Two days later, *Il Messaggero* carried another report.

'Was servant baby killer threatened?

'Rome, 12 January. Police are still guarding the hospital where Massimina Meleschi, accused of infanticide, is being held.

'Yesterday the police were able to interview the domestic servant who remains in a serious condition. Meleschi cries almost continually, with momentary pleas for help followed by fits of anger against a man she hasn't yet named. The police therefore interviewed her at the earliest opportunity. The woman admitted giving birth around 6 a.m. on the morning of 8 January to a baby boy and intentionally allowing it to die by depriving it of the necessary care. The woman seems also to have stated that a man, still unidentified, threatened her on several occasions. The man is thought to be the father of the child and his threats, compounded by the man's own mental state, may have led the woman to commit this insane act.'

I eventually found my body again, my knees, and also the night, after my mind had been reassembled through the effect of the different visions and this other shock. I found the corners of my room again and the dimension of my presence in the centre of things which I had always had and felt like another part of me, and which I had to move and induce and improve as a part of myself—each exact thing, even in the laws of my science, bringing some comfort, which anyone who is mad cannot have, since anyone who is mad through bodily sickness heads towards death with every gesture and fragment and hair and scale and opens a black mouth and utters meaningless words and suffers and cries and goes killing, seeking to die and totally disappears, since his machine has understood that its course has now ended and has no choice but to give in.

All exact around me, space and time too, all together in the ribbon of my memory, in the gentleness of my hands and of my tongue, under the cover of my brows and of my forehead; all together, peaceful, devoted to bettering my fate through thought and learning, confidence and study; all together in progress to arrive at the invention of a better machine and a better environment in which nature can itself sense the meaning of going forward along a straight line and not repeating its phases according to the rhythm of death and of apparent rebirth.

In *Il Messaggero* I found yet another report.

'Massimina Meleschi Crocioni, the servant arrested several days ago in Via Uruguay on a charge of infanticide and concealment of a corpse, has made a signed statement to the police from her hospital bed. According to her declaration, the male child, born on the morning of 8 January at the house where she lived in Via

Uruguay, was the child of her lawful but estranged husband, one Crocioni, resident in the Marche. According to the woman, Crocioni had abused and ill-treated her for many years so that she was forced to leave the matrimonial home and take work in Rome as a servant.

'The reasons for this ill-treatment are to be sought in the eccentric personality of Crocioni, who claims to possess certain pseudoscientific truths, which he stubbornly champions and defends, to the point of endangering her life and that of her family, spending money on fruitless investigations and neglecting every marital responsibility. Crocioni had seen his wife many months before, making threats if she refused to return to live with him, and on that occasion, at night, he violated her. The woman was so disturbed by her husband's continual ill-treatment and by his latest threats that she was driven to a state of hysteria. For all these reasons she became convinced that her husband is a madman who is a danger to himself and others. The woman finally justified her action by stating she had preferred in such circumstances to let her newborn son die rather than see him grow up under the shadow of the father and with the risk that he might inherit the same mental disturbances.'

Madness or instability or confusion of the senses or loss of reason, sickness of the brain or of the heart, incapacity to recognize oneself, rejection of oneself and others—that is certainly something quite different from my own, from my freedom, and it is the least free thing that exists, being enslaved to the world of Massimina, of the consigliere and of the judge, of the prosecutor and employers and managers, whoever they might be: a fundamental training ground for ignorance of this society, since madness is the bullying of the consigliere, the meanness of the police, the justice of the judge, just as madness is the poor stupidity of Massimina who thought she could rebel by going to work as a servant in Rome, or of those who believe in money, in the power of their tyranny and in the organization of their misdeeds.

But anyone who is mad offends himself, and I have certainly never offended myself, nor have I ever thought of doing so. Anyone who is mad offends himself by trying to take a part of others, that same part that offends in itself, and which he doesn't want others even to have, to acknowledge and to exercise: pure freedom, research, knowledge, the way of moving ahead, looking, inventing and fearing nothing and not flailing in the fear that around there is only a great spectacle of death.

Those who are mad play a role they have found through the convenience of this offence they wish to give to themselves and to others—a role carefully rehearsed and given to them by the society in which they continue to play their part. In fact, if you look at these madmen, you'll see they are all identical in their madness and all do the same things. Society depends on the presence of these poor madmen and on their incapacity to say a word different from what they usually say, and to see the small changes that old age produces on the stage and behind the scenes and therefore on the face of this society and on the society it represents, and the scars inflicted on them beyond old age, the currents that move from other stars to our planet, in the fond attempt to stir its mortal sky; and to see the mysterious hypocrisy that invests and envelopes it like a black cloud and which flies like a gas that contaminates everything.

I have found my consciousness again and I move between my rooms, and since I have now decided to return to my project of the statuette and to get out of this world, which is a true seat of madness, I do not see the spectacle of death around me, which yet darkens and contaminates the senses of those who have isolated me and have chosen to reject me. Even now I am ready to join up with them, and to lead them, and be led, to hold Massimina's hand and kiss her pallor on her murder bed. I would still not believe in death, even if I had the cardboard box with the corpse of my son inside. I would unwrap that newspaper, if Massimina were watching me, in the hope that she had hidden a flower or a bud inside. To be able to embrace Massimina over this cardboard coffin and return with her to guide the clouds of San Savino, the fields, and my machines.

I still don't believe in death, even if I've chosen to make use of its passage. I see no spectacle of death even in this grim winter that stands before me, not even in the obscurity of these two or three days that separate me from the explosion. If I see a sparrow, I think of its flock and of how they fly, and if I see a poor little oak bent down by the snow, I think how in March it will suddenly shake itself free, and that the sparrow and the oak can be freed by the shortness of their destiny and of their happiness with the establishment of a system which brings each, at the end of its course, to a place further on than the place from which it began to move.

I went out in front of my house and had the feeling that things might follow me. I waited a little longer and ate something. I never used to wait, nor am I waiting now for those poor things to happen that Massimina wrote about in her letter, and which have already happened everywhere and even at San Savino—wait for your master to set you free or pay you more; wait for his Excellency to die or to mend his ways or to be fooled, once he is sitting senile in his armchair; wait for the priests and professors to tell you the truth; wait until you're old and have no need of anything; wait until time, this enemy kept in a cage, can comfort you by repeating its songs. I'm not waiting. I've decided to move forward. In this book I want to write down my last actions in the attempt I'm still making to move forward.

I went out in search of money. I went to Liborio but he had nothing I could steal. I took the motorcycle and went to the sulphur mine to look for a stick of dynamite. I spoke to the store manager and said I needed the dynamite to blow up some vines. He sent me to a foreman who made me wait two hours and then gave me a stick of dynamite for 2,000 lire. 'Be careful, friend,' he said, 'be sure you blow up only what has to be blown up!'

'You're right, friend,' I replied, 'I'll blow up what I have to.'

I left the store and went back to San Savino. I took back the motorcycle and returned home. But winter is beautiful, and perhaps because I'm now in mid-air and away from all the concerns about the land and its system, I can now look once more, in a way I had never looked before, straight at everything and with such fondness;

a sparrow or a young oak, but also the great oaks and then the edges of the fields, the lanes, the stones that emerge from the snow, the flattened brambles, the animal tracks, puddles and springs hidden under the great blanket and which re-echo in a non-existent void and will last just a short while, the duration of one frost or one gust of wind. Darker clouds behind Montevecchio, a streaked sky behind Acquaviva, everything magnified at Frontone. The houses, with their window eyes brought close by time and by one fixed thought. I am proud and happy, and in this pride I think that no one—at least no one in San Savino, nor even I believe in the Marche or in Italy—has ever attempted what I have tried to invent and to do. It doesn't even matter if my work is lost, since nonetheless it was an important achievement in the cause of progress. I think my science has to be worked up, now that I'm in mid-air and away from every concern, from art and from poetry, even if a few days ago I wrote that contemplation and representation are no more than a petty intoxication of feelings, the repetition of them and the desire to stop everything, and therefore to reject science; and that all of this is naturalistic and artistic.

Today, however, I can say that poetic feeling, which is artistic vision, is itself also an instrument of science, or that science can have two heads just as easily as twenty thousand or two million heads, and I think that the happiness of free machines is an artistic happiness, which progresses through the work of those who make it progress. In that same moment in which it thrives and progresses, in which one makes and enjoys, through creation.

I move on and come to a hedge and then to a steep climb called Il Ciuco, then the houses where the Baluganti live, then those of

Stortino, Ciarafone's wide valley. For me, these places and these names, at this moment of immense freedom, have the same value as my first hopes.

I've come further on and have reached Monte Cupello and seen where the woods start again, as far as Monlione. I have seen a few patches of earth among the whiteness of the snow and the sky. Then, since the light was changing, I saw a whole north-facing hollow still white and powdery, covered with frost, dark violet on that maternal evening. In this hollow and its crystalline lights, I saw the extension of each thing, of its essence, of its force. I saw how the image divided and multiplied and I realized that in my life, I had expressed, in full conscience and with sufficient freedom and purity, the infinite progression of every particle and molecule and body, and I had achieved a scientific result with my own life alone, with the construction of the ideas that have sustained it. A so-called concrete result, or any other proof, would have been just another fact for this society: it would have instantly captured them, then turned them to stone.

I, instead, have left a bright start that is heading through the sky like the tail of a comet. In a few moments, once it has crossed this horizon at Fossombrone, it will be already visible from Montegiove, above Fano, and then from Rimini and then from Bologna, and will go around like these stars that now shine and which a few hours ago were over America.

I made a snowball and sucked it. When I reached the edge of the open ground in front of my house, I found a flock of thrushes perching on the usual rosemary bush and the ivy on the elm. They ruffled their perch when I arrived, causing some snow to fall, but luckily none of them flew away. I returned upstairs and put the dynamite inside the statuette. I went down for a drink and then to close the doors of the house. I went to get the measures of gunpowder and prepared the charge and the primer. I now know how the statuette will explode. I don't yet know whether I'll hold it tight against my chest or my forehead or under my chin or if I'll rest the back of my head against it, stretched out on the bed.

I hear some noises and must go to the window to look. The night is all purple, human, but it is clearing in colour and draining into the hollows and crags. I feel it losing a weight, a formless sorrow behind the mountains.

Everything, every material, is turning rigid and the space between my window and the door behind me is now dense through the impression I have always felt from the coldness around. I have only to leave this window, turn, cross the room, and go upstairs. Now I'll begin.

———

AFTERWORD

In *The World Machine*, Volponi has created what one critic described as 'surely one of the most bewilderingly pathetic figures in contemporary Italian fiction'.[1] Anteo Crocioni is a self-taught rustic philosopher, a wife beater, a deluded man at odds with everyone around him. All his energy is focused on a techno-utopian vision that he is setting down in a treatise entitled *For the Constitution of a New Academy of Friendship of Qualified People*, which he hopes to publish and present to university professors in Rome and in foreign universities. In it he lays out the notion that people are machines built by other machines and that the true destiny of mankind is to build ever-more sophisticated machines through which society will become more alive and free.

In pursuing these ideas, he leaves his land uncultivated and alienates himself from all those who might have helped him. He abuses his wife, scorns her family, steals from his neighbours, rejects the authority of the Church, offends politicians, and when he finally reaches the university in Rome he is met with incomprehension.

---

1 R. L. Clements, *Saturday Review* 50 (49) (9 December 1967), n.p.

We can see that the story will end badly, even from the early pages when we read the allegations of ill-treatment against his wife in the court proceedings against him. We follow events through Anteo's eyes but soon recognize him to be an unreliable narrator. His wife is the victim of his abuse, and we await his downfall.

And yet we are caught in the closed world of his mind, following his misguided utopian dreams for a better society, his obsessions about a world governed by science, where technology might offer an escape from poverty and the drudgeries of manual labour. Here perhaps we find some grounds for sympathy.

The novel is set in central Italy of the 1950s and '60s, in an area that was still struggling to emerge from almost medieval feudalism. The Marche region had been formed from the Papal States after the Unification of Italy in 1870, but the Church remained a power to be reckoned with, particularly in rural areas.

Most of the land was parcelled into farms owned by the Church or by landowners such as Mordi. Each farm was little more than a few fields, cultivated by tenants under the *mezzadria* system by which all produce—grain, cattle, wine, cheese—was divided equally between tenant and landowner. After a good harvest, a farm might yield enough to feed the family that worked it, but a lean year brought hardship, sometimes starvation, while landlords would take their half share just the same.

The land was still ploughed by hand, with oxen. The first tractors didn't arrive here until the mid-1950s. Old farmers today can still remember the exact size of each field and how many days it would take to plough.

The priest or landowner oversaw farms through a manager, or factor, who was responsible for dividing the produce. There was no security of tenure. If a family did well, they were promoted to a larger and more profitable farm, while those judged to be less efficient or who incurred the disfavour of the priest were banished to a smaller, poorer, or remoter farm.

The Crocioni family had been fortunate in having their own land, though it must have been inadequate since Anteo's father had a job as Mordi's manager.

Despite his many delusions, Anteo's ideas about the future of agriculture were not so ill-conceived. Small landowners needed to jointly invest in modern machinery and this, indeed, is what would soon happen. In the 1950s such visions were considered too revolutionary—too 'Bolshevik'—for the likes of Mordi who, instead, misspent his agricultural loans from the government and went bankrupt.

The 1950s marked a watershed. Just as the first tractors, balers, and threshing machines were arriving in San Savino and other parts of the Marche, farmers were tiring of the struggle to subsist and had started looking for a more comfortable life elsewhere. The family Anteo met on the train and the woman who sold lupini beans were among the many Marchigiani who had moved to Rome. Others travelled abroad to find jobs in the building trades in Switzerland, in Belgian coal mines, as garbage collectors in the United States, or on the Canadian prairies. In the face of this exodus, with more and more farms left deserted in remoter districts like Monlione, land values plummeted and owners had little option but to sell to their tenants, through mortgages, for whatever they could get.

The post-war years marked a period of political turmoil. Mussolini's downfall in July 1943 after twenty years of Fascist rule had led to civil war in all but name. By the end of the Second World War, Italy was financially ruined and had to start again. The king had been too closely associated with Mussolini and the monarchy was replaced by a republic with a new constitution.

The end of fascism was not marked by great trials like those in Nuremberg after the fall of Nazi Germany but by arbitrary justice. Mussolini and many of his followers had been publicly lynched and further revenge killings followed. Many fascist officials or sympathizers discreetly withdrew from public life, while younger fascists found jobs in the forestry corps or the police force.

The influence of the Church was still strong. It had played an ambivalent role in Italian politics during the 1930s, but the end of fascism left a gap that had to be filled. The new political force came from the Catholic-inspired, centrist Christian Democratic Party (Democrazia Cristiana), established in 1943. Its major rival was the Italian Communist Party (Partito Comunista Italiano), whose core membership had fought to bring down fascism. It had played an active governing role in the early years of the new Republic but was viewed with suspicion.

By the 1960s, with the gradual spread of Russian-style communism and with membership of the Italian Communist Party now over a million—making it the largest communist party per capita in the capitalist world—the Church threw its weight behind the Christian Democrats, preaching against communism and threatening its supporters with excommunication. This political polarization would lead to civil unrest—the so-called *anni di piombo*, or years of lead—which reached a peak in the later years of the 1960s and the early '70s.

Paolo Volponi was born in Urbino in 1924, two years after Mussolini's March on Rome, and spent his whole childhood under the shadow of Fascism. His novel *The Javelin Thrower* (*Il lanciatore di giavellotto*) gives a vivid portrayal of Italian life during this period, telling the story of a disturbed young adolescent who witnesses his mother's love affair with a local Fascist commandant.

Volponi graduated in law from the University of Urbino in 1947. A year later, he published his first collection of poetry, and won the prestigious Viareggio Prize in 1960. He continued writing, though his career took a decisive turn through his meeting with the industrialist Adriano Olivetti. In 1956, Volponi joined Olivetti in Ivrea, north-west Italy, becoming his head of human resources and righthand man. They collaborated on one of the most enlightened industrial projects in 1960s Europe in which industry was seen as a centre of development and education for its workers rather than just a means for private profit. This notion, considered by some to be dangerously socialist, placed Adriano Olivetti under CIA surveillance.

Olivetti's company had been manufacturing typewriters since 1908 but was now experimenting with electronic calculators and computers. The earliest computers were the size of wardrobes, but in 1965—the year that Volponi was writing *The World Machine* (*La macchina mondiale*)—Olivetti had launched Programma 101, one of the first commercial programmable desktop calculators, opening the way for the arrival of the first computer. The technological implications were already apparent and a new utopian vision of the world seemed not far away.

Volponi published his first novel *Memoriale* (*The Memorandum*) in 1962. He laboured for the next two years on a second novel (later published as *La strada per Roma*) but suddenly abandoned it. On 9 November 1964, he wrote to his friend Pier Paolo Pasolini: 'Now I have to stop all work on this novel and hope to begin the third, about the farmer with philosophical ideas.'[2]

The reason for this change of plan was his encounter with Pietro Mario Vallasciani, an eccentric fellow Marchigiano, who had arrived at the Olivetti factory in Ivrea to work on the construction of electronic calculators.

As Volponi later explained: 'I made the acquaintance of someone who came from certain Marche hills, though from the southern Marche, not the *Marca* of Urbino. Why to Ivrea? Because research was being done in Ivrea on new machines, on calculators, and he had an idea that men were machines built by beings who had come to Earth, had built man like an imperfect machine and had left him to his destiny.'[3]

2 Archivio Bonsanti, letter number 60, in Paolo Volponi, *Romanzi e prose*, VOL. 1 (Turin: Einaudi, 2002), p. 1105.
3 Paolo Volponi, 'Incontro con la Pantera' in *Scritti del margine* (San Cesario di Lecce: Piero Manni, 1994), p. 182.

Volponi's wife would later describe him thus: 'Vallasciani was a small, self-educated man, talkative and rather fanatical: reminiscent of a certain old-fashioned cultivated anarchist. He came to visit us several times in Milan. I was once able to look at one of his pages: very confused and barely comprehensible.'[4]

Volponi's meeting with Vallasciani had an enormous impact. He set to work immediately, dictating his new novel to a secretarial typist, and within a few weeks had produced a draft manuscript of 322 pages, which was subsequently corrected by hand and amended with further typewritten pages.

Volponi's papers, now at the Fondazione Carlo e Merisa Bo in Urbino, include a 33-page typewritten copy of Vallasciani's treatise. Parts of it appear in the novel, including the diagram on page 139.

A friend of Volponi recalled that Vallasciani 'had swamped the world with that treatise, had sent it to universities, to science institutes, to professors of cybernetics in Italy, the United States and elsewhere. Some had taken it seriously, the University of Bristol, the Massachusetts Institute of Technology in Boston, then it all came to nothing and P.M.V. felt himself a victim of fate.'[5]

In Volponi's novel, extracts from Vallasciani's treatise appear in italics. They have little or no scientific basis, his scientific notions are illogical and readers are expected to lose their way in the labyrinth of poor Anteo's mind, an effect reinforced by the narrator's poetical reveries.

---

4 Giovina Volponi, conversation with Emanuele Zinato, Milan, 10 June 1999, in Volponi, *Romanzi e prose*, VOL. 1, p. 1111.

5 Corrado Stajano, 'Il capitale umano di Volponi', *Corriere della Sera*, 2 February 2014.

What is the translator to do? Readers of the Italian edition have direct contact with the author and can read Volponi's lyrical prose. A translation, however, is mediated by another voice and the translator might have good reason to worry that the reader will mistake a stylistic eccentricity in the original for a poor translation. I have sought to remain as loyal as I can to the original, looking for meaning where it can be found and making sense so far as possible. But most of all I have worked on the sound of the translation, attempting to follow the rhythm and sound of the original. This has sometimes led me away from the actual words of the text in search of an effect more consonant with the voice and poetical spirit of the original.

It is no coincidence that Volponi chose to name his protagonist Anteo, after the figure in Greek mythology. Antaeus was the half-giant son of Poseidon, god of the sea, and Gaia, goddess of the earth, and lived in the Libyan desert. He challenged his opponents to wrestling matches and always won by pinning them to the ground, remaining invincible so long as he remained in contact with Mother Earth. His final and fatal contest was with Heracles, who realized he couldn't beat him on the ground and so lifted him high and crushed him in a bear hug. The parallel is unavoidable: once Anteo Crocioni had lost touch with the land beneath him, his fate was sealed.

Richard Dixon